Lin Man-Chiu is a well-known children's author in Taiwan who has published a number of successful YA novels as well as non-fiction titles. In Taiwan, she received the Golden Tripod Award for children's fiction in 2003 and the "Good Books Everyone Can Read" Award for the best children's book of 2010.

The Ventriloquist's Daughter was longlisted for the 2014 Found in Translation Award and subsequently selected for the *Found in Translation Anthology*.

Helen Wang is Curator of East Asian Money at the British Museum, and a literary translator working from Chinese to English. Her translations for children include *Bronze and Sunflower* by Cao Wenxuan, *Jackal and Wolf* by Shen Shixi, *Pai Hua Zi and the Clever Girl* by Zhang Xinxin, and *Tan Hou and the Double Sixth Festival* by Cai Gao. She has also translated short stories by a wide range of Chinese authors. She is the Winner of the 2017 Marsh Award for Children's Literature in Translation.

LIN MAN-CHIU

The Ventriloquist's Daughter

Translated from the Chinese by

Helen Wang

balestierpress

Balestier Press
71-75 Shelton Street, London WC2H 9JQ
www.balestier.com

English edition published by arrangement with Global Kids Books,
a division of Global Views-Commonwealth Publishing Group,
through Rights People, London

First published in English by Balestier Press in 2017

ISBN 978 1 911221 05 0

The Ventriloquist's Daughter

1

A Postcard From Afar

We were expecting Baba. Instead, we received a postcard from him, with a message saying:

Gone travelling. When I get to the end of the road, I'll turn around.

I was with my grandparents when it arrived. Yeye was furious. He hurled the postcard to the ground. "Don't bother coming back!" he shouted.

After Mama's death, Yeye had paid for Baba to go to America. He had sent him to do an advanced medical course, not to go travelling.

Nainai's face filled with sorrow. "Where is the end of the road?" she muttered to herself.

But I was delighted. The postcard was addressed to me!

Baba had been overwhelmed by Mama's death. He didn't talk. He didn't eat. He just sat by her grave, his face buried in his hands, his beard overgrown and his hair long and tangled. His eyes were like caves, dark and sunken, dull and lifeless. I'd never seen such a sad face, drained of all hope.

Yeye couldn't stand his dejectedness, and urged him to pull himself together. But Baba didn't seem to hear. Eventually Yeye grew angry. Exasperated, he insisted that Baba go back to work at the hospital.

"What kind of doctor am I, if can't even save my own wife?" Baba replied coldly.

"Kai Xiang, it wasn't your fault that Shui Ye died." Yeye spoke softly. "It would have made no difference if Ming De had done the surgery. If Shui Ye could hear you now, she wouldn't blame you."

"She would! She would blame me!" Baba's voice was like the roar of a wild animal. "I'm a doctor and I didn't even know she was ill! And even if she didn't blame me, I'll never be able to forgive myself."

Then he burst into tears. "I let her down. I'm responsible for her death."

Yeye's tone changed. "Pull yourself together," he said crossly. "Men don't cry."

Nainai was annoyed too, but she tried not to let it show. "Kai Xiang, try to get a grip on yourself," she told him gently. "Your father's not getting any younger and the future of the hospital depends on you."

"Ma, can't you see? I'm not suited to being a doctor! If you put the hospital in my hands, it'll be a disaster."

Yeye flew into a rage: "You lazy good-for-nothing! Look at Ming De—he works hard and takes his responsibilities seriously. If you were half as conscientious as him, there wouldn't be a problem."

"I told you to let him have the hospital. I'm trapped here. You won't let me leave. If you'd let us go our own way, live our own lives, then Shui Ye would still be here."

"And what would you be living on? Without our support, Shui Ye wouldn't have died of ill health, she'd have died of hunger." Yeye's face was black as thunder. "You don't know what's good for you. You're a waste of space." He stormed off.

Nainai let out a big sigh and followed him, leaving Baba in the depths of his sorrow.

I'd been crouching behind the door, out of sight. I waited until Yeye and Nainai had gone, then quietly went to Baba. I didn't know what to say, so I just pressed against him gently.

Baba glanced at me, his lips quivering as though he was going to say something, but before the words could come out, there were tears rolling down his face.

"Don't cry, Baba," I said, wiping them away.

He wrapped his arms around me and mumbled in my ear, "Liur, be a good girl; don't make a fuss, just go and play."

"Only if you'll play too," I said, in a baby voice.

He sat there, stiff and numb. "Be a good girl, and tomorrow I'll buy you a doll."

"Really?"

He nodded. "Tomorrow I'll go to work and I'll bring home a doll for you, I promise." Then he reached his little finger towards me to make a pinky promise.

I thought he would cheer up and pull himself together after that. But he didn't.

He went from bad to worse. He started drinking.

The atmosphere at home was heavier than ever. Yeye's face grew tighter and tighter with the strain. Nainai's expression was clouded with worry. It went on for over a month.

Then Yeye put a stop to it, by sending Baba away.

I'll never forget that day. Our housekeeper Ah Fen came to pick me up from nursery. On the way home, she said, "Hurry up, Liur, your baba's about to leave."

I panicked, pulled my hand away from hers, and ran home as fast as I could.

When I got there, I was gasping for breath. Baba was just about to get into the car. He flung his arms around me and held me tight.

"Where are you going?" I asked, my heart pounding inside my chest. "Tell me where?"

He didn't say a word. His face was streaked with tears.

Yeye pulled me away from Baba, saying, "I'm sending him to the USA on a training course. It's very difficult for him to get back on his feet here."

I didn't reply. I could feel my heart shattering into little pieces.

Yeye told Baba to get in the car. Baba took a couple of steps forward, then came back and hugged me. "I'll bring you a present," he said, choking through his sobs.

When Baba left, my heart went with him. I became very quiet and the only time anyone heard my voice was when Qing Qing came to the house.

Qing Qing and I were closer than sisters. She was Uncle Ming De's daughter. He and Baba had played together as children. The two of them had grown up together. Ming De's family had not been well off, and Yeye had helped him go to medical school. Since graduation he'd been working in Yeye's hospital. He was very close to our family.

After Baba left, Uncle Ming De was even kinder to me than before. Auntie looked after me too, and often sent Qing Qing over with nice things to eat. How lonely I would have been if they hadn't been there.

"What kind of present do you think your baba will bring back for you?" Qing Qing asked me one day.

"A doll," I said, without having to think.

"How many dolls do you want?!" she asked. "Didn't he buy you one with blonde hair and moving eyes for your birthday?"

I stared into the distance. "I didn't ask for one, but I have a feeling that's what he'll bring back."

"When's he coming home?" she asked.

I shook my head. I didn't know.

Baba had sent us a letter as soon as he arrived in America, but after that we had heard nothing. Yeye wrote to him many times, but Baba didn't reply. At first, Nainai would say, "America's such a big place, it's bound to take ages for a letter to arrive." But as the months went by, she started to fret. Yeye was worried too, but reassured himself that his son must be very busy on the course, and didn't have time to write home.

I continued to hope that the postman would bring us news from Baba. But the days came and went, and still there were no letters. In the end, Yeye could stand it no longer, and made a long-distance call to America to try and get some information. That was when we learnt that Baba hadn't even lasted the first month—he'd dropped out.

Yeye was furious. Nainai was worried sick. I didn't know what to do with myself. Where was he? What if something had happened to him? Yeye asked someone to find out, but his contact drew a blank.

At this news, Yeye's face crumpled. Nainai sighed. I felt completely lost.

That autumn I started at primary school. I felt anxious about everything. Then Baba's postcard arrived, and I began to relax. I knew only a few characters and couldn't read what Baba had written, but I was so happy, and full of hope that there would be another postcard soon.

Every month or so after that, I received a postcard from Baba. Often, he simply told me where he was. Sometimes he didn't write anything at all. I wanted to ask Yeye to read what was written on the postcards and tell me where Baba was, but I did not dare; Yeye was still angry. He didn't want to know about the postcards. He didn't even look at them.

When he learned that Baba had gone travelling, Yeye started spending even more time at the hospital. When he was at home, he stood staring silently into the forest at the back of the house, frowning. Nainai did the same. I heard them talking a few times, saying that Baba wasn't coming back, and discussing what they should do about the hospital, and things like that. But mostly I just heard them sighing under their breath.

I could understand their sadness, but I didn't want to comfort them. They had never comforted me. In their eyes, I was just a girl, and a girl couldn't carry on the family business. I hated them for giving Baba such a hard time, and for putting so much pressure on Mama to produce a son. If I weren't a child, I'd have run away, just like Baba.

I couldn't run away but my heart was with Baba, and I followed him through his postcards. They consoled me when I was sad and missing him. They also opened my eyes: before the end of first grade, I could name some of the states in the USA and knew that Mexico was a separate country.

One day a postcard arrived showing a man, with his heart ripped out, lying on a stone slab, surrounded by a group of people half-kneeling in worship. I was terrified. There was no message, so I ran straight over to Qing Qing's and asked Uncle Ming De where the postcard had come from.

He said it was from Mexico, that the picture showed an Aztec sacrifice, and that it was an Aztec custom to offer human hearts to the gods. He told me about Aztec religious practices, and about local customs and traditions in Mexico. And he showed us some photos of Mexico, scenes that were so different from anything I'd ever seen! The houses were different, the forests were different, even the people looked different. I put the photos in front of the photograph of Mama, and told her,

"Baba's been to such unusual places. Look, this house is made from dried cactus!"

I was interested and curious about Mexico, but the idea of human sacrifice filled me with fear. Night after night, I dreamt about Baba being captured and tied up on the sacrificial altar, the priest holding up a sharp knife, ready to slit open his chest, remove his heart and offer it to the gods. I would scream in my sleep, sometimes so loudly that I woke Nainai.

Qing Qing knew I had nightmares, but she didn't comfort me. Instead, she laughed. "Didn't you hear what my ba said? When the Mexicans were under Spanish rule, they became Catholic, so there aren't any human sacrifices now."

I knew I was taking it too seriously, but the thought continued to trouble me.

Although the postcards could never put my mind at rest, they sent ripples through the heavy atmosphere around me. When Baba left Mexico, I followed his postcards and toured the islands of the Caribbean, then south to Guatemala, Costa Rica, Nicaragua, Cuba, Haiti. Places I had never been became important to my life. I spent ages staring at the postcards, thinking about Baba travelling there, and the yearning inside me grew and grew: one day, I would travel to all the places he had been, and experience them for myself.

During the summer holiday after second grade, Yeye had a stroke. He had been as fit as a fiddle all his life, but now, paralysed down one side of his body, he couldn't talk properly and spent all day lying in bed, becoming more and more cantankerous. He would bang on the bed frame and shout, but Nainai was the only person who could understand him.

A few months later, Yeye had another stroke. He slipped into a coma and was unconscious for several weeks. Uncle Ming De said Yeye was waiting for Baba to come home before he could die. When Nainai heard this, she was overwhelmed with sadness and could not contain her tears.

In the end, Yeye didn't wait for Baba. He died in the hospital he himself had built.

Without Yeye, the house felt even more deathly quiet. It was a big house, and there were only a few of us: me, Nainai, Ah Fen and Mr Chen, the driver. Nainai asked Ming De to look after the hospital and spent her days reciting Buddhist sutras. She seldom paid any attention to me. I carried on as I had before, going to school and back everyday.

And it was then that I started to explore the forest behind the house.

2

A Purple Skirt

I knew the forest well, but to be there on my own was an adventure. The excitement of my wanderings distracted me from the bleakness of my life and the forest's tranquillity soothed my lonely soul.

For as long as I could remember, I had walked here with Baba and Mama. I would dart about like a rabbit, guided only by my mother's singing. She loved to sing and her voice was sweeter than a lark's. I loved listening to her.

I preferred to talk than to sing, delighting in everything I saw and heard and felt.

"Mama! Listen to that little rabbit over there in the grass—it's coughing like an old man!"

"Baba! Can you see those wild strawberries in the cracks between the stones? They're whispering to each other!"

All day long I would chatter like a sparrow, until Mama couldn't stand it any longer. "Even the trees would cover their ears, if they had hands!" she would say.

I would hang my head in embarrassment and keep quiet for a few seconds, but then I'd forget myself and start talking again.

Then it would be Baba's turn. "And if the trees had feet, they'd have run away by now!"

I would smile sheepishly and close my mouth, but before a minute had passed, my crisp, loud voice would be ringing round the forest again.

The forest was at the back of our house, part of the family estate passed down from our ancestors. Nainai always said that we owed our wealth to the benevolence of our forebears. My great-great-grandfather had started the family line in healing people and saving lives. He founded the family hospital, which, by the time it passed down to my grandfather, was the best in town. But Yeye was keen to develop it further, and wanted my father to expand it, make it bigger and better. Unfortunately, Baba didn't have the same kind of drive as Yeye; he wasn't ambitious.

My father also seemed to me more of a poet than a doctor. When we walked in the forest, he would pluck beautiful words from the air. When he saw a bird feeding her newly hatched chicks, he would be more excited than I was. When he saw blossom blowing about in the air, he would wrap his arms around Mama and dance. When he saw that all the autumn leaves had fallen, his eyes would mist over. I was aware of his sentimental nature from a very young age. One smile from Mama, and he would be happy all day. One sigh from Mama, and he would frown with worry. Countless times I heard Baba telling Mama that he would love and cherish her all his life. Back home, the pressure from his parents dragged him down, but, here in the forest, he could truly express his love for her.

Mama was also romantic, but living in a small-town doctor's family was not easy. She was often in tears, and when I asked what the matter was, she would simply say, "If only you were a boy!" or something like that. Nainai had also said it countless times. I didn't understand: weren't they female as well? Why did they want me to feel that being a girl was such a terrible thing? On one such occasion, I couldn't help adding, "I want to be a doctor when I grow up too!" Nainai had cast a cold eye at me. "Even if you were a doctor, you'd still be female!"

Mama was under enormous pressure to produce a son. The year I turned four, she was finally pregnant again. The family was overjoyed with the news and so was I, until Ah Fen said something that filled me with fear:

"Liur, when your little brother is born, no one will love

you any more." She said it with such menace.

I didn't care if Yeye and Nainai gave all their attention to my little brother, but I couldn't bear the thought that Mama would stop loving me.

From the moment she became pregnant, the frowns and scowls disappeared from Mama's face, and I could see a difference in the way Nainai treated her. I was convinced it was Mama who was looking forward to the birth of this little boy the most, and that she was going to give all her love to him. Whenever this thought came into my head, I started to panic. I was sure Baba would ignore me as well. Now that Mama was pregnant, he no longer hugged me first when he came home from work, but rushed straight to Mama, like a doting servant. He had changed, and I was filled with jealousy and anxiety.

As Mama's belly grew bigger, that nameless terror grew deeper inside me. In my dreams, the unborn baby bared his teeth and showed his claws. He stole my toys, demanded my bedroom, robbed me of my parents' love. I became an unwanted orphan, living downstairs in the servants' quarters with Ah Fen.

I started playing up. The more I tried to attract Baba's attention, the more it backfired. Everyone was sick of me, even our ginger tabby cat started picking on me. Then, perhaps God took pity on me or something, because my tragic fate changed. Mama had a fall, a fall that shattered the hopes of everyone in the family. After six months in the womb, the unborn baby boy we had all been waiting for lost all signs of life.

The threat was gone.

I had Baba's attention again, maybe even more than before. But Mama did not love me more than before. The miscarriage hit her badly. I rarely saw her smile now. And Nainai denied her smiles to Mama.

When Mama felt better, the three of us—Baba, Mama and I—went for walks in the forest again, and I ran around like a rabbit, just as before. Except that Mama didn't sing any more. She started nagging, constantly telling Baba that we should move out and live in our own place.

At first, Baba tried to soothe her, but as time passed, he retreated into silence. This irritated Mama, and she became increasingly short-tempered. After one particular outburst—"You never do anything. You won't take the initiative,"—Baba, helpless, gave just one response: "I'm an only child. I can't turn my back on my parents." And then he turned and walked away, back to the house.

After that, Baba stopped coming for walks with us. He spent less and less time at home, going to the hospital first thing in the morning, and not getting home until after dark. Sometimes I'd be asleep when he came back.

Then, one night, I was woken by the sound of him shouting. Quietly I pushed open the little door at the side of the wardrobe that led to my parents' room— my parents had paid for someone to come and knock through the wall when I was born so they could be closer to me—and I saw Baba lying spread-eagled on the bed, his face pale and thin. Mama was sitting in the armchair by the window. She looked heartbroken.

"I'm tired. Leave me alone." Baba pulled the covers over his head.

Mama didn't move. I watched an enormous tear roll all the way down her face.

After that, the atmosphere in the house was suffocating. Mama grew thinner and thinner. She stayed in her room, and didn't speak or come downstairs to eat. Sometimes, she would look at me strangely and mutter, "If only that child had lived." Her mind was full of the son who had died. She couldn't see the daughter who was alive and in front of her eyes.

It was like being punched all over again. I did my best to avoid Mama, and clung to Baba instead. As soon as he came home from work, I was in his arms, pestering him to tell me stories, taking up every minute, every second, of his time. He loved it when I was daddy's girl. He played silly games with me, and listened to my childish stories.

In my eyes, he was the most amazing father in the world, and he in turn told me that I lit up his life, that no matter how troubled he was, his worries vanished into thin air as soon as he saw me.

One day, he sighed and said with great feeling, "I wish you didn't have to grow up."

At the time, I didn't understand what he meant, and answered, "People always grow up. It's only dolls that don't."

"Then you can be my doll," he smiled.

"But I don't want to be a doll! I can't wait to grow up."

"When you grow up, you can't do the things you like to do," he replied. "What's good about that?"

I knew that Baba didn't like being a doctor, so I told him I didn't want to be a doctor either.

Baba suddenly looked at me very seriously. "You must have the courage to pursue your dreams. Don't let anyone make you do otherwise. Don't let anyone try to change you, OK?"

I nodded, but I didn't really know what he meant.

But what he said next took me completely by surprise. "Your mother's changed, Liur. She's just like Yeye and Nainai now, always trying to make me do things I don't want to do. It drives me mad!" He hugged me tight. "You're the only one who isn't on my back. If it weren't for you, my life would be unbearable."

I felt embarrassed. Sometimes I'd feel bad for Mama about spending so much time with Baba, and I'd make a big show of wanting him to go and be with her. "But you all like boys, and I'm not a boy," I said.

"Thank goodness you're not." Baba stared at me. "If you were a boy, there would be too much pressure on you. I want to you have a wonderfully happy life." There was sadness in his voice.

"But Mama is a girl. Why is she so unhappy?"

"Because…" Baba broke off. After a pause, he continued, "You're still little; you wouldn't understand."

I dropped the question, and started chattering about school. I could chatter on about anything. I would tell Baba everything that happened at kindergarten that day, every detail from start to finish; I would sing him the new song I had learnt, or try to make him laugh. As my relationship with Baba grew closer, my relationship with Mama grew more distant. It wasn't that I didn't spend time with her, just that we rarely talked about ourselves. Her troubles weighed heavily on her. I wanted to comfort her, but was afraid that she would talk about my little brother again. And I was scared of that sad look in her eyes. So unless she called me, I'd stay in my room, playing by myself.

One day though, Mama fainted. I was terrified. Fortunately, she soon came round and I asked her if she was ill.

She shook her head. "It's nothing," she told me. "You mustn't tell Baba."

I was confused. "Baba's a doctor, why won't you tell him?"

Mama's gaze drifted towards the forest in the distance, and, in a faint voice she said, "Don't disturb him."

The sadness grew deeper in Mama's face. The only time I saw her smile was when we walked in the forest. Perhaps it was the magic of the place, or the feeling of relief at leaving the house, but Mama started singing to me again. One particular day, the forest was quiet and I was caught up in a game—watching a wild rabbit until it ran out of sight, then following a dragonfly as it danced through the air—when the sound of gentle laughter rang out. From the corner of my eye, I saw Mama leaning against a tree, her shadow within the shadow of the tree, extending over the ground, and her long purple skirt fluttering in the forest like a butterfly.

I ran over to see my friends the ducks. The show they created at the edge of the marsh gave me endless delight. As soon as the black duck heard my call, it pulled its head out of the water. It took such a pride in its appearance, yet the feathers on its head were always out of place— every time it caught its reflection in the water, its little eyes would look pained with dissatisfaction. Then there was the pair of mandarin ducks, exceptional dancers, always spreading their wings, leaping and dancing by the water's edge. A mother toad swam by, with a little toad on her back, its eyes half closed as though in a beautiful dream. Suddenly I heard a cry. Startled, I looked round and saw a mother duck trying desperately to save her duckling's life. It had wandered away and was playing at the edge of the marsh; when an eagle swooped down, hungry for a meal, the mother duck rushed in, grabbed the duckling's foot in her beak and yanked her offspring under the water. The duckling, taken by surprise, was protesting loudly. The moment its head bobbed up, the mother duck pushed it underwater again. She did this several times. The duckling learned its lesson. The eagle gone, it waddled off comically beside its mother, drawing its head and neck close to its body. When it had recovered its confidence, I crouched down and gently stroked this little dusky yellow ball of softness. It pecked at the palm of my hand, and then at my feet, which made me giggle.

It was while I was enjoying myself beside the marsh that I heard a cry in the forest. I ran as fast I could and when I saw what had happened, I froze to the spot. Mama was lying on the ground, her face whiter than the lotuses beside her. I called her name and shook her, and she managed to splutter a few words:

"Go and get Baba!"

I raced home to get help. Mama was taken to hospital, but she never came round. My shock concealed my grief. How could she be dead? Only a few hours earlier she'd been walking in the woods with me. What had made her so ill? The family was engulfed in pain, and no one answered my question.

Mama was buried in the forest, wearing her favourite purple skirt. On the day of the funeral, Baba wept constantly. I stared blankly at the purple skirt, as beautiful as lilac blossom. Afterwards, Yeye had Mama's things removed from the house, worried that they would be painful reminders for Baba. All I was left with was a pile of old photos. Mama looked so beautiful and happy in the photos, quite different from the Mama I remembered.

I would often look at the photos and ask myself: *Was this beautiful woman really my mama? What could have made her become so pale and so thin?* Later, when I was allowed to go to the forest by myself, my relationship with Mama became more intimate. Perhaps it was loneliness, a need to talk to someone, but whenever I went for a walk, I would always go first to her grave. If only I had spent more time with her, I thought. If I had tried to be closer to her, maybe she would have had a happier life. Standing in front of her grave, I realised how much I needed her. By then, Baba had left me, but Mama was still here in the forest, and whenever I missed her I could go and see her.

Unlike Baba. If it weren't for the postcards, how would we even know if he was still in this world? As I stood by Mama's grave, watching the leaves fluttering in the breeze, it seemed that in every one of those leaves I could hear her singing, and see her purple skirt, as beautiful and as delicately fragrant as ever.

3

The End of the Road

In fifth grade, during the winter holidays, I received a postcard from Baba showing a village with mountains in the background and the sea in front. The sea was blue and the sky was blue, and the high mountains were covered in snow. I asked Uncle Ming De where this place was.

He read the small print on the back of the postcard. "It's Ushuaia, the southernmost city in Argentina. You can't go any further, except into the sea, so people call it 'the end of the world'."

As I heard 'the end of the world', I froze. Qing Qing jiggled my hand. "Liur, what's the matter?"

I could barely contain the joy in my heart. "Baba's coming back."

Qing Qing looked at the postcard, which was blank on the back. "How on earth do you know?"

I started to smile, and without explaining, repeated, "Baba's coming back! He's coming back!"

I ran straight home and told Nainai. She made a noise in the back of her throat, a non-committal kind of noise. I didn't care whether she believed me or not. Baba had said that when he reached the end of the road he would come back.

Then I ran to the forest. The wind was behind me. The birds were singing in the trees. The scent of the trees filled my nose. I was smiling from ear to ear and shouted all the way, "Baba's coming back! Baba's coming back!"

I ran to Mama's grave, emptied the little vase, and refilled it with freshly picked purple flowers. Sweat poured from my brow, running over my grinning face. When I'd finished, I made myself comfortable by the grave and, my heart bursting with joy, cried, "Mama, he's coming back! Baba's coming back!"

I repeated the words over and over, oblivious that dusk was falling, its golden glow quietly covering the forest.

I waited and waited, my heart filled with joy. I stopped going to Qing Qing's house after school, and stopped going to play in the forest. I sat quietly in the garden at home, waiting. Qing Qing waited with me. We moved a table into the garden, so we could do our homework while we waited. I wanted to be there to welcome him as soon as he appeared. I only had to hear the sound of a car on the forest road and I would spring to my feet.

Even the sound of footsteps made me restless. I was desperate to walk in the forest again with Baba, to stroll by the marshes together, to take a lotus flower for Mama. I recalled all those nights when I couldn't sleep, when I'd stood by the window looking at the stars, thinking about Baba so far away. Silently, in my mind, I had said to the stars, Tell him I'm thinking of him! As I grew up, I stopped telling my thoughts to the stars, and started to learn about them properly. When I was small, Baba would lift me up in his arms and tell me about the constellations and planets: he'd show me The Maiden (Virgo), and point to where the King of the Otherworld (Pluto) lives, but now I could distinguish them for myself; when Baba was back, I would surprise him. I would sing for him too, just like Mama used to. I knew I'd never be able to sing as well as Mama, but Baba loved to listen to her, and he was bound to like my singing too. Mama had tried to teach him, but he couldn't get the notes right, and had given up. "It doesn't matter if I can't sing," he told her cheekily. "I'll always have you and Liur to listen to!" Thinking of Mama, my eyes began to sting.

I waited and waited. But as the first signs of spring crept into the forest, there was still no sign of Baba.

"How come he's still not back?" Qing Qing asked me.

"He's coming back from the end of the world; it's

bound to take time," I said.

My eyes fell upon the last postcard. It was such a beautiful place! Ushuaia—the letters were printed in white on the blue sea, as though they were swimming or flying. When I looked at those letters, my heart began to soar too. I looked for it on a map and, as Uncle Ming De had said, it was the southernmost town in Argentina. The only direction the road could run was into the sea. We'd learned that Ushuaia had been a place of exile for criminals, and that later, because of its location, it became a departure point for boats going to the South Pole. Now, as well as scientists, it was teeming with tourists. Quite unexpectedly, it had become a tourist destination. When Baba got there and discovered it was the end of the road, of course he would turn round and come home.

"Maybe your ba went to the South Pole!" said Qing Qing.

"Even if he kept going and went to the South Pole, as long as he keeps going, he'll still come home. Isn't the teacher always telling us that the earth is round?" I said with total confidence.

"So why is it taking him so long?

"I guess he can't afford the flight home. If he has to come by boat—you know how big the Pacific is—it could take him months to get here!"

Qing Qing agreed. After a while she asked, "Do you

think he'll bring you a doll?"

"I stopped playing with dolls ages ago."

"Have you forgotten? You said he would bring back a doll."

I remembered what Baba had said as he was leaving. "Well, he probably doesn't know how much I've grown." I suddenly started to worry. "What if he doesn't recognise me? I was so little when he left; I hadn't even started primary school."

"Of course he'll recognise you, Liur. My ma says you look more and more like your mother. She says you've got her eyes. There's no way he won't recognise you."

Qing Qing's words reassured me. In the torment of waiting, time dragged so slowly. The atmosphere at home was as heavy as ever. Nainai never said a word to me about Baba, but quietly asked Ah Fen to prepare my parents' bedroom, to buy new curtains, bedcovers and wardrobes. I knew Nainai was looking forward to Baba's return too.

But the days passed, and there was still no sign of him, not even a postcard. I started to get impatient and anxious. "Could something have happened to him?"

Qing Qing comforted me. "Of course not!"

"Perhaps he's been captured by pirates?"

Qing Qing laughed out loud. "Well, only if he really is coming by boat, and even then, it's unlikely he'll come across any pirates."

I blushed. I laughed at myself for worrying that the sky might fall in. But I couldn't keep it up for long. Soon I started worrying again. "If he goes north from Argentina, he'll have to cross the plains of Patagonia. What if he stumbles across a ranch and gets shot? That's what your ba said, isn't it, that all the farmers on the Patagonian plains have guns and bodyguards, and that they open fire on strangers."

"Yes, but he was talking about the past. That was decades ago. These days, you go to prison if you shoot someone, so it doesn't happen any more!"

"But there's no water on the Patagonian plains, and there are no trees. If there isn't a farm for twenty miles, what if he collapses on the road?"

"Remember what my ba told us: nowadays, lots of people go travelling on the Patagonian plains, and there are plenty of cars and tourist buses on the roads. If he did collapse, someone would find him."

Thank goodness I had Qing Qing, otherwise I would have scared myself to death with silly ideas.

From the beginning of May, the weather started to get hot, and I moved my table to a shady corner of the garden. Although I was out of the sunlight, I could still feel the oppressive heat burning into me. Ah Fen urged me to go inside. I pretended not to hear, and continued to sit there waiting. I waited with such patience, but as time passed by, despair and frustration took root inside me. I was angry with Baba, and I was angry with myself. If he'd forgotten the promise he'd made five years before, then what kind of fool was I for waiting? One afternoon, I was so upset that I pushed over the table and ran, furious, into the forest.

A ribbon of red cloud split the turquoise sky, then dispersed into countless red balls that rolled across the sky. As I watched the heavens, gradually my fury and frustration dispersed with the clouds.

"You idiot," I told myself. "Why are you waiting for him? He's forgotten about you. He's forgotten about his family."

My hope too dissipated like the clouds, disappearing one thread at a time. *Let go of your dreams,* I told myself. *He has forgotten what he wrote on that first postcard. He doesn't want to come back, and perhaps he never will.*

I ran through the forest, not noticing that dusk was falling around me. Instinct led me towards Mama's grave. Then I froze as if an electric shock had run through me. A man was standing in front of the grave. Two days earlier, Ah Fen had seen a tramp while she was walking in the forest, and told me to be careful. Perhaps this was him? Her words had made me feel angry and violated. I might not have been there while I had been waiting for Baba by the house, but it was my forest! How dare anyone trespass? I would be merciless to any trespasser I came across! But when I saw him now, I felt scared. What if he tried to kill me? Or rape me? I wanted to run, but my feet wouldn't move. My eyes fixed on the tops of his shoes. They were covered in dust. He must have walked a very long way. Then suddenly, an idea came into my head. It was a stupid idea, a ridiculous idea, but I was riveted by it. My heart was in my throat, the arm holding my bunch of flowers was numb, but I kept my eyes on those dusty shoes. It was a crazy, ridiculous idea, but I was powerless against it. With my heart in my throat, and holding my hand with the flowers aloft, nice and straight, I kept my eyes on those dust-covered shoes and slowly moved forward.

The man had long, thin legs, draped in beige trousers, and chocolate-coloured arms that glistened in the sunlight. His body was like an earth-coloured stick, tall and lean. Starting from his feet, I gradually followed his body upwards. I wanted to see his face.

His head hung low, his face screened by long hair and a hat. I stared at him. Sweat was pouring from me. My T-shirt, soaked and clinging to my body, rose and fell with my pounding chest. I was rooted to the spot. Eventually, he leaned forward, picked up a suitcase from the ground beside him, and without raising his head, turned and walked away. I remained exactly where I was, my mind filled with that idea. Was it him? How could it be? The Baba I knew was an educated, good-looking man, who held himself well and kept himself smart. He didn't look like a tramp.

And yet, I had this strange feeling. I walked over to Mama's grave. "Is it him? Has he come back?"

Her response was the same as always, the sound of the wind in the trees.

I stayed by her grave until dusk had settled around the forest. Then I turned and headed home. But before I'd set foot in the garden, I heard a dog barking. The black cat that liked to crouch on the low wall let out a shrill cry, and leapt into the grass as though running from danger. And the big tabby cat arched its back, as if preparing to face the enemy.

The dog wouldn't stop barking; there was clearly something bothering it.

"What is it?" I asked the animals. I was unnerved too.

They couldn't answer, of course, but instinct told me that a stranger had come to the house. My heart was racing. I looked at the front door, but I dared not open it. I knew that whatever was behind that door would be life-changing. I longed for it to be Baba, but I was scared of my own prediction. Ah Fen heard me and came out. She looked me in the eye in a strange way, and said in a low voice:

"Your baba's come back, Liur."

My mind went blank, and my body froze to the spot. Ah Fen hesitated, then finally took my hand, and said, "Let's go in."

I could feel a booming in my forehead and, stepping as though my feet had lost consciousness, I shuffled after her. Once inside, my eyes scanned the living room. He was standing with his back to me. I couldn't see his face and I didn't need to. As soon as Nainai saw me, she stood up, and without saying a word, hurried upstairs. There was red around her eyes; she had obviously been crying. By the time I looked back at him, he'd turned around and was facing me. As our eyes met, the smile vanished from his face. I was taken by surprise, and stared like an idiot at his dust-covered shoes.

Never in my dreams had I imagined it might be like this—that after waiting such a long time, we would be meeting as strangers.

That evening, Nainai didn't come down for supper, and Baba fell asleep on the sofa. Ah Fen took me into the kitchen, and said quietly, "Your nainai said not to wake him, but to let him rest." She brought me a plate of food, but I had no appetite.

The crescent moon had crept into place and the stars were twinkling in the night sky. I stood by the window, overwhelmed with sadness. Baba had changed. If I'd met him on the street, I wouldn't have recognised him. He was dark and thin, and his clothes were old and worn. No wonder Ah Fen had thought he was a tramp. But it wasn't his appearance that shocked me most; it was the look in his eyes. I'd looked for Baba's tenderness, but had seen a coward, desperate to escape. I suddenly felt scared: I had waited such a long time, such a very long time, for him to come back, but Baba was no longer the person of my memory, the person who had feelings for me and who loved me.

That night, I dreamed of Mama. She was running through the forest, her lilac skirt floating through the grass, and Baba and I were chasing after her. When we reached the marshes, her lilac skirt turned into a waterlily, a lilac cushion surrounded by lilac petals, slowly drifting away. There was a little boy sitting on the cushion. Panicked, I turned towards Baba, and found a face full of pain and sadness. Baba waded into the marshes, his arms reaching out in front of him, ready to pick up the child. As the boy drifted further away, Baba went after him, the deepening water coming over his knees, then his waist, then his back. The boy kept drifting, and as Baba's head slipped underwater, I screamed, "Baba! Baba!"

Then someone was by my bed, gently patting my back. When I opened my eyes, I saw the face I'd waited so long to see.

"Baba!"

"Shh!"

Baba put his finger to my mouth, motioning me to sleep. With him there to protect me, I slipped quickly into the land of dreams. I was back in the forest, but this time I was lying happily in his arms, rocking gently, as if in a boat on the calmest lake. I was so happy, floating free in this sea of love. Such pleasure! Such peace! I smiled and opened my eyes to check that I really was in my baba's arms once again. But there was no one there, only the stars twinkling in the window.

Had Baba really come? Or was it a dream? I lay in bed, sadness washing over me again. Then, vaguely, faintly, I heard a sound coming from the room next door. Was Baba still awake? Was he talking to someone? Without thinking, I got up and went over to the side of the wardrobe. I hesitated, then quietly opened the little door into Baba's room. I hid myself behind it, and peered through the crack.

It was dark inside, and although I couldn't see Baba, I could hear his voice. "Carola, we're home. We're home at last." His tone was soft and warm.

"This isn't my home. I want to go home. Take me home." It was a little girl's voice, high and silly.

My heart skipped a beat. I knew Baba hadn't brought

anyone with him. So who was that talking to him? Then everything went quiet, and all I could hear was my heart pounding away.

After a while, I heard Baba's soft tone again. "We have to stay here, this is our home."

"Carolo, are you drunk again? You know my homeland —there are snow-covered mountains and turquoise lakes, and cacti and alpacas. How can this place be my home?" She sounded angry.

"Carola, don't get mad. I promised you, didn't I? I will take you back, but not right now."

There was a sound of seashells scraping together, and a voice expressing displeasure. "You said you just wanted to see her. Well, you've seen her now, so why can't we go?"

There was silence again.

What they were talking about? Why did she call Baba "Carolo"?

Then the girl started up again. "Carolo, you can't stay here. She will make you sad. Haven't you noticed? They're so similar; they're almost identical. You have to get away, otherwise your heart will break again."

"That's enough, Carola, don't say any more. Please don't say any more." Baba gave a long sigh, and the room went quiet again.

I stayed hidden behind the door. There were so many mysteries floating around in my head. Who was Carola?

When did Baba change his name? And what kind of relationship did they have?

I didn't sleep that night. In the morning, I got up as usual, and made myself ready for school. All was quiet in the room next door. Baba must still be in bed. Before leaving the house, curiosity got the better of me and I opened the little door again. I did it very carefully and very quietly. It was dark, but in the pale light shining through the curtain, I could see that Baba was still sleeping. I could see a wooden box, but I couldn't see the girl called Carola. Had I been dreaming the night before?

I decided to find out and opened the door a little wider. Apart from Baba, who was sleeping, there was no one else there. How could that be? What on earth was going on? I stood there like an idiot. But as I was preparing to leave, something caught my eye. It was just as I had imagined five years previously.

Baba had brought a doll back for me.

4

The Talking Doll

As soon as I arrived at school, Qing Qing rushed over to me and asked excitedly, "So your ba's back then?"

Her question caught me off guard, then I realised that Nainai must have phoned to tell Uncle Ming De.

Qing Qing was ready with her next question. "Did he bring you a present?"

"A doll." I smiled at her.

"He really did bring you a doll!" Qing Qing's face lit up. "What kind of doll?"

"You'll know soon enough." I kept smiling.

"Still playing with dolls at your age? Everyone will laugh at you!" Qing Qing giggled, poking fun at me.

"It's not an ordinary doll, you'll see."

"Tell me, tell me, what's it like?"

I'd wanted to keep quiet, but Qing Qing kept pestering me, and after school I described the doll to her.

"Its face looks a bit like dough that's been left too long —it's rough and dry, and starting to go brown. Its eyes are black glass balls. They're dark, but they don't catch the light. There's a nose you can barely see, but the mouth really stands out; its lips are bright red, as if someone's just put lipstick on them. Its hair and ears are covered in a woolly cap—the kind they wear in Peru, with ear flaps, that we've seen in books. But this woolly cap's special: it's old and has a different kind of pattern, and it has two tassels that hang down from the ear flaps, like brightly coloured sweets. They're very pretty and you can't help looking at them."

"What kind of clothes does it wear?"

"It has a red-brown cape. In one hand it holds a flute, and on the other it wears a shell bracelet, and there are straw shoes on its feet…"

That day I was not the only one distracted at school; Qing Qing was itching to know more.

I told her about seeing Baba in the forest, and what happened when he came home. I told her every little detail. The only thing I didn't mention was the voice I'd heard in the night. It was obvious that no one else had been in Baba's room, so there couldn't have been a girl's voice. I must have dreamed it.

Qing Qing was excited about going home with me after school. She said she wanted to say hello to Baba, though what she really wanted was to see the doll. And so did I.

I was bursting to talk to Baba. I had so much to tell him. And I wanted to bring out all the postcards, so he could tell me about every single one of them: what he did in those places, what his life had been like. I was so eager to learn about his experiences during the years he'd been away, but whenever I was near him, I'd start to feel uncomfortable. I didn't know why.

Baba was sitting in the garden when we got home. He had his back to us. He didn't seem to notice that we were there. I wasn't sure whether to call out to him or not. Qing Qing looked at me. She was clearly shocked by his appearance.

"It doesn't look like him" she mouthed.

I didn't make a sound. My hands were clammy. I didn't know why I was so anxious.

And then I heard Baba speak.

"That's the lilac tree I'm always telling you about. It's beautiful, isn't it?" His voice was even gentler than I remembered.

"It's pretty, but cacti are more beautiful." It was the girl's voice!

My reaction was electric. Immediately, my eyes were on him. But there was only Baba. There was no one else.

Qing Qing looked bewildered.

I was finding it hard to breathe and my feet were trembling.

"There are so many beautiful flowers here, I'm sure you'll love them." Baba's voice was gentle and calm.

"Even if I like them, I still want to go home." It was the girl's voice again, this time accompanied by the sound of shells jangling together.

Then Qing Qing asked: "Uncle Kai Xiang, who are you talking to?" And as soon as the words were out, she gasped in surprise. "Ah! So this is the doll you were talking about, Liur?"

For a moment, Baba's eyes caught mine. I wanted to call out his name, but the look in his eyes frightened me —a look of panic. Then, just as quickly, he looked away.

I stepped forward, and saw he was holding the doll in his arms.

"Who are you?" asked the doll, its mouth neither open or closed, its black glass eyes glinting in the sunlight.

It was the same voice I had heard in the night.

I shot a glance at Qing Qing. How could a doll be talking?!

"Carolo, these girls are so rude. Why won't they answer my question?"

In a flat voice, Baba gave the reply. "The darker one with short hair is Liur, the one I've told you about. The girl with plaits is her best friend Qing Qing."

"SO THAT'S LIUR?!" the doll exclaimed, firing its beady eyes on me. Then, in a tone of contempt, "I thought you said she was beautiful. What's beautiful about *her*? Look how dark she is; she's been out in the sun too long. Oh, I see! She's a wild child who plays out all the time."

It was as though I'd been punched. I felt my face go red. My whole body felt wrong.

"How you can say that? Apologise right now!" said Baba.

"Sorry, I was joking." The doll faced me and bowed, its shell bracelets jangling as it did so. Then in a childish way, it said, "Hi, Liur, I'm Carola. You can call me Auntie Carola."

I was still feeling uncomfortable, when Qing Qing started to laugh. "Carola, can you really speak?"

Carola turned to Qing Qing. "What kind of question is that? If I couldn't talk, how could the two of you hear my voice? Idiots!"

"Carola, do you have to be so rude? Where are your manners?" said Baba.

But Qing Qing wasn't angry. She looked back and forth between Carola and Baba, until eventually the penny seemed to drop. I could see on her face that she'd found the answer, so I looked too—and found the answer for myself.

Carola couldn't speak; it was Baba who was speaking, as a ventriloquist.

Over a year ago, Uncle Ming De had taken us to see a film about a ventriloquist, who travelled to the four corners of the earth, performing with his doll. Qing Qing and I had loved that film, and we had loved the ventriloquist's doll. Qing Qing had found some photos of the ventriloquist's doll in a movie magazine, which she had kept and treasured.

My eyes went back to Baba while Qing Qing stared at Carola, the ventriloquist's doll. The doll's head turned and, in a tone of irritation, it said, "What are you looking at? What's so interesting?"

It was the first time I had seen someone speak without moving their lips.

Qing Qing's eyes were wide open too. Baba's ventriloquist skills were totally convincing.

Carola was getting impatient, and rattling her shell bracelet. "Qing Qing, you came to see Carolo. Well, you've seen him, and you can go home now."

"Carolo? You mean Uncle Kai Xiang?" Qing Qing giggled. "Oh, I didn't come to see him! I came to see you. We've been waiting five years, and now I've seen you at last."

"You've been waiting five years? What do you mean?" asked Carola.

"Five years ago Liur told me that her baba would bring a doll back for her. And sure enough, Uncle Kai Xiang has brought a doll back. Don't you think that's amazing?"

Baba's gaze drifted towards me. Although he glanced at me only for a moment, I could see joy in his eyes.

"Huh," scoffed Carola. "It was probably a lucky guess. What's so special about that?"

Qing Qing was still grinning. "Of course it's special! And a few months ago, Liur said her baba was on his way back home. No one believed her, not even her nainai, but here he is! Either she has supernatural powers or the father-daughter bond is very special."

I saw a glimmer of delight in Baba's eyes, but still he didn't utter a sound.

The question came from Carola's mouth. "How did she know?"

Qing Qing turned to me. "Liur, it's better if you tell them!"

I could feel my heart beating in my chest. Timidly, I said, "Because on his first postcard, Baba wrote, 'When I get to the end of the road, I'll turn around'. So when I got his postcard from Ushuaia, I knew he'd be back soon."

I looked at Baba. His face was twitching, as though he'd just had a shock. It seemed he didn't want anyone to notice; he held Carola up high to hide his face.

Carola rattled her shell bangles. "Do you know where

I come from?"

Qing Qing answered, "South America. Peru, isn't it?"

Carola clapped her hands together, and jumped up and down, "That's right! That's right!"

I was feeling more encouraged now, and I blurted out, "Where there are snow-covered peaks. And barren places without any trees. And there are alpacas, and cacti everywhere. Your houses are made of mud-brick and dry cactus branches. And you eat cactus leaves and alpaca as well, don't you?"

"And there's Machu Picchu," added Qing Qing, "the ancient city of the Incas, that they built two thousand metres up in the mountains, with over one hundred flights of steps, each made from a single stone slab. No one knows how the Incas managed to move such heavy rocks up the mountain all those centuries ago."

"There are lots of towns built three thousand feet up in the mountains. My favourite is Cuzco, the jewel in the crown of the Andes. There's a lot of Inca remains and Spanish architecture, and the people there wear traditional clothes and play the panpipes." These were all things I'd seen on Baba's postcards.

"How do you know so much about Peru?" asked Carola.

"Whenever Liur got a postcard from Uncle Kai Xiang, she'd come over to my house and ask my baba. He'd tell us all about the places, and sometimes he'd set us a task, ask us to go to the library and find a book about a particular country. We loved doing that, and we learned a lot about South America. My ba used to say that the postcards were like a geography text book for us," said Qing Qing.

"And I thought nobody cared about those postcards!" said Carola.

"Oh, but we did! Liur treasured those postcards. She never let anyone touch them. Once, I accidentally splashed one of them with my fizzy drink, and she was so mad she wouldn't speak to me for a week!"

"But there was almost nothing written on the postcards," said Carola. "Why on earth would you treasure them?"

"They had my name written on them!" I didn't intend to say any more than this, but I was so excited I couldn't hold back. "I checked every day to see if a postcard had arrived, and if a couple of months went by without one, then I'd get worried. I was so scared that Baba might have fallen ill, or come across bad people. And I was scared he'd forgotten about me, and might never come back." I spoke quietly, my eyes finding Baba.

Baba hid his face behind Carola's body, and I couldn't see his expression. Carola didn't say another word.

For a while the atmosphere became stiff, and then

Qing Qing asked, in a deliberately relaxed way, "Uncle Kai Xiang, how do you make the girl's voice?"

I opened my eyes wide. I wanted to know the answer too.

Baba's mouth didn't move, but Carola shuffled a bit and said proudly, "He has such a horrible voice, how could he make a girl's voice? If you listened carefully, you'd know that everything I just said came out of my own mouth, and had nothing whatsoever to do with him."

Qing Qing persisted. "But how can a cloth doll talk?"

Carola rolled her eyes, leaned forward and said in a low voice, "I have magic powers."

"You're joking!" Qing Qing laughed.

"I'm not joking. You can ask Carolo!" said Carola.

We turned to look at Baba, who glanced away. He didn't look anything like a ventriloquist who spoke through a doll.

"If you really have magic powers, put out your hands and let us see!" Qing Qing challenged him.

"I'm using magic powers to talk to you right now!"

"How can you say that's magic? If it weren't for Uncle Kai Xiang, you'd just be another doll, wouldn't you?"

"Whether you believe it or not is up to you." Carola gave a cunning smile.

"You can't fool us—can she, Liur?" Qing Qing looked at me.

I didn't say anything, but looked quietly at Baba.

His face was still hidden behind Carola, as though he wasn't there at all.

Then, all of a sudden, I had a strange feeling—that Carola really could talk. I was beginning to believe it —that she wasn't a cloth doll, but a real child. It was as though I could see emotion in those glass eyes; as though when our eyes met, I could see a provocative, arrogant, disdainful look.

I gulped, shocked at my response. How could I be so gullible?

5

Burial Goods From Ancient Tombs

Two days later, we were invited to Qing Qing's house for a special meal.

Auntie's wonderful cooking filled the table. Everything looked, smelled and tasted superb. Uncle Ming De brought out a bottle of good vintage and toasted us enthusiastically. Baba was quiet, and it took a few drinks before he started to open up. He told us all about his travels and adventures, and how he became a ventriloquist.

"I was carrying so much sadness and grief, drifting from one city to the next. I couldn't tell you how many places I'd been or what I'd seen along the way. Everywhere was the same; I just wanted to be able to numb the feelings inside me, to forget the grief. The pain of losing my wife was something I couldn't come to terms with.

"I wandered like a restless ghost. If I was hungry, any

bit of bread would do. If I was tired, I'd fall asleep the moment I lay down.

"One day, I found myself in a remote village in the foothills of the Andes. There was no food in my backpack. Even my water bottle was empty. I was hungry and thirsty, and walking like a robot. As the last light of day slipped behind an adobe wall I could hold out no longer. I saw a wizened head appear in a doorway down the side of the wall, and then I collapsed.

"I don't know how long I was out for. I heard lots of voices, male and female, old people, children. There must have been a whole family living there. I wanted to thank them, but there was no strength in my body. I couldn't even sit up. I thought I must be ill. I lay in bed, listening to them talk in a language I had never heard before. I didn't understand what they were saying, but I felt it was a good atmosphere. I decided it must be a very happy family. But then the happiness reminded me of the past that I was trying to forget, and I slipped back into the pit of grief. And I realised for the first time how deep my grief was.

"I stayed there for a few days, and the strange thing was that they left me alone all that time. It wasn't that they weren't looking after me, otherwise there wouldn't have been a hunk of bread on the little table by my bed every morning, together with a cup of green liquid. I don't know what the substance was: it tasted bitter and made my nose sting. At first, I didn't dare to drink it, but I was so thirsty, and the bread was so dry and hard, that I forced myself. It was only later that I learned it was a local remedy. After drinking it for a few days, I started to get my strength back.

"When I was finally able to get out of bed, I wanted to go and thank the family. From the doorway, I looked into the room opposite and saw a group of people sitting with their backs to me. From where I was standing, they seemed to be children. I said hello in a quiet voice, but no one responded. I felt a bit embarrassed, then after some hesitation, I went over to them.

"I took one look and began to laugh out loud. They weren't children at all, just some cloth dolls. They were about half child height. I don't know if I was fully conscious, or imagining things, but I saw one of the cloth dolls open its mouth and call me: 'Baba, Baba'. It touched a nerve, and I crumpled into a corner and wept uncontrollably."

When I heard this, my eyes started to mist over. The atmosphere in the room was charged with emotion. Baba silently drank his wine. Nainai looked alarmed. No one in Qing Qing's family said a word.

After some time, Baba carried on:

"Then, one afternoon, I saw that wizened head again.

The old man was hauling a big sack into the house. He saw me and, without saying a word, went into another room. I didn't move, but sat in my corner, looking out of the window, watching the sunlight creep up the mountain. As the last ray of light slipped over the top, I noticed that he was standing in the doorway, looking at me enigmatically.

"We stared at each other for a while, then the man turned and walked away. But he soon came back, and this time he had a cloth doll in his arms. As he walked towards me, I heard a child's voice. I couldn't understand what was being said; all I could catch was 'Carola, Carola'. I looked around in surprise—there weren't any children in the house. The old man made the doll raise its hand and point to itself. I heard the child's voice again and looked in astonishment at the old man. His mouth hadn't moved! And a cloth doll can't speak! Then I realised, he was a ventriloquist."

Baba had had the same reaction to the ventriloquist as I had when I heard Carola's voice for the first time that night. It was a very strange experience.

Baba told us more about the old man's house. His name was Uchu, and he was Peruvian.

"Behind Uchu's house was an expanse of open land. The sky is an intense blue, and the earth an intense red. It seldom rains there, but once it starts, columns of water burst from the sky—they are big and fast, and come thundering down with a terrifying noise. When they hit the red mud, they create the most beautiful sprays of water. To the east of the house is a bare mountain, where nothing grows but cacti, and which reaches across the horizon like a screen, cutting off the villages and towns on the other side.

"Uchu had lived alone there for decades, barely interacting with other people, with just a few cloth dolls and some cats to keep him company. But there was always a lot of activity. He used his skills as a ventriloquist to make the dolls talk among themselves. He was a perfect mimic and could speak in a wide range of voices: male, female, young and old. Occasional passers-by had the same impression I had when I first came across his house —that there were lots of people living in it!"

"Did you learn to be a ventriloquist from him?" Qing Qing's brother asked.

"Yes, he taught me while I was staying with him, and chose the name Carolo for me. Six months later, I set out with Carola, the cloth doll he had given me, as a travelling performer."

"Isn't it strange that such an eccentric loner should have taken you in?" asked Auntie.

"It was fate," said Baba, "I couldn't even speak to him. He was an Indian, and spoke a tribal dialect. I didn't understand a word of it, but the strange thing was, we seemed to make sense to each other."

"If you couldn't communicate with him, how did he teach you to be a ventriloquist?" asked Uncle Ming De.

"That—" Baba turned away, so we couldn't see the expression on his face "—is something I can't tell you."

"I believe this person called Uchu must have had a whole set of special powers," said Auntie. "But I'm intrigued to know how a middle-aged man like you can produce a young girl's voice?"

"If I tell you that when I hold Carola in my arms, something happens that lets me forget my natural shyness and awkwardness, and allows me to become another person, would you believe me?"

"In terms of performance psychology, it's quite plausible," said Uncle Ming De. "Many actors forget themselves when they're on stage, and switch completely to being in character. I can believe that the same is true for ventriloquists."

"I don't know anything about performance psychology. All I can say is that I couldn't perform without the strength I draw from Carola. I couldn't do it without her," said Baba, looking visibly more relaxed.

"It sounds so mysterious, as though Carola has some kind of magic power," said Qing Qing's brother.

Qing Qing and I put down our chopsticks at the very

same time and stared at Baba. Nainai did the same. Baba
didn't utter another word, and for a moment there was
tension in the air.

"Anything's possible—South America's full of magic!"
Uncle Ming De laughed, and encouraged us to eat.

Baba took a sip of wine, and began to tell us about
his travels after leaving Uchu's house. I couldn't keep up
with what he was saying, as my mind was still on what
had come before. As Baba told it, there were almost no
trees in Uchu's village, just cacti and beautifully coloured
rocks. The villagers wore the traditional clothes of the
Inca people. They ate alpaca meat, chewed on coca
leaves, and walked barefoot among the cacti. It was hard
to believe that Baba had lived there more than half a year,
and had learnt ventriloquism from someone he couldn't
even have a conversation with. It was like something you
might read about in a fairy story.

While I was lost in thought, Baba quietly placed a
piece of meat in my bowl. I was overwhelmed by this
unexpected gesture and my whole body froze.

Qing Qing nudged me. "See, your ba adores you!"

I was inexpressibly happy. Auntie saw it in my eyes
and said with feeling, "Liur's got her doting father back
again. Isn't it lovely!"

Tears welled in my eyes. Qing Qing shook her head at
me. I lowered my head and wiped them away with my

hand.

Uncle Ming De looked like he was trying to remember something—which came to him all of a sudden. "I saw a report in an archaeology magazine saying that an archaeologist working at six thousand feet in the Andes had dug up a mummy of an Inca girl. What was she called? Ah, yes, I remember: Juanita. There was a photo of her. She was beautiful. She had long, raven-black hair and wore a poncho made of alpaca wool. She looked very serene. It was hard to believe she'd been dead several hundred years already. Did you see her on your travels, Kai Xiang?"

"Yes, I saw her in a museum in Argentina. And she is beautiful. She was sitting curled over as though she was sleeping. There are a lot of other mummies like her. They voluntarily offered themselves to the gods—that's why they look so peaceful," said Baba.

"That's what it said in the magazine," said Uncle Ming De. "But some people doubt that they went voluntarily. The way Juanita grips her clothing with her right hand suggests she was scared and struggling."

Baba took a sip of wine, and said coolly, "Of course she'd be scared, like anyone who's walking to their death. But there is no greater honour than to be a messenger between your people and the gods. She would overcome her fear, offer herself and prepare for the journey. It was a romantic and spiritual choice."

"The children were so young though. Did they have much of a choice?" There was disapproval in Uncle Ming De's tone. "It sounds good to say 'offering', but in fact it was an exchange. The parents fattened their children up, led them to the sacrificial altar, and as a reward they got a hefty payment. It was very calculated."

"There was compensation, yes, but it's impossible that they did it entirely for the reward. They loved their children, like parents everywhere—but they were willing to forsake what they loved most for sake of the tribe. Even the children regarded it as an honour. They took the blessings of the tribe, and walked bravely and proudly into the arms of the gods. They went happily to their death and there is no suggestion of pain on their faces."

"They were brainwashed!" Uncle Ming De was getting worked up. "The magazine said the children who had been chosen thought they were going to heaven—so of course they were happy, and chose their favourite dolls to take with them. They had no inkling of where they were really going. The most moving thing is that they thought the road to heaven would be long, so they took two pairs of straw shoes with them, never imagining that the shoes wouldn't even touch the ground! If those children had known that 'going to heaven' meant going to their graves, I doubt any of them would have been willing to go. Traditions like that were so cruel."

"That's because you don't understand their beliefs."

Uncle Ming De had more to say, but Auntie stopped him. "All this talking! Have some more food!" Then, as a generous hostess, she selected morsels of food from the different dishes and placed them in my bowl.

There was silence as we started to eat again. Then, out of the blue, Qing Qing asked, "Uncle Kai Xiang, Carola's very old—was she found in a grave?"

In an instant, all eyes were on Baba, including mine.

Baba's tone was matter-of-fact. "All of Uchu's cloth dolls came from burials, including Carola."

I felt a shiver run down my spine. Qing Qing was stunned too. The atmosphere became tense again.

Baba raised his glass slowly and took a sip.

Then, Qing Qing's brother spoke. "Uncle Kai Xiang, it'll be the Water God Festival soon, would you like to show everyone what you do?"

"Ah, the Water God Festival, I'd completely forgotten about it! In Peru, lots of villages have a water god festival. I'm sure Carola would be delighted to perform at one here."

Nainai slammed her chopsticks on the table. "What do you think you're playing at?" she raged. "Haven't you wasted enough years already? You'd rather be a ventriloquist than a respectable doctor? You know full well what your family expects of you. Like a fool, your father waited for you to return so he could hand the hospital over to you before he died. We never expected you'd be so reckless—that you'd be gone so many years. And now you've finally come back, all you can think about is performing. What about the hospital?"

Auntie was quick to calm Nainai down. "Kai Xiang's only just got back. We can talk about all this in a day or two. Don't start on him now."

Uncle Ming De took over. "Kai Xiang, I must hand the hospital over to you. I've been waiting a long time for this day to come."

Baba's face turned very serious. "I won't be going back to work. I'm not going to be a doctor again." He paused then said, "Ming De, could you arrange the performance for me, at the Water God Festival?"

Before Uncle Ming De could open his mouth, Nainai was railing again. "If you're not going to be a doctor, then what have you come back for?"

Baba's gaze drifted towards me, then quickly away again. "I shouldn't have returned," he sighed, then he stood up and left the room.

I followed him out and called to him—but he ignored me. Holding back my tears, I stood in the doorway of Qing Qing's house, watching Baba as he disappeared into the night.

Qing Qing came and stood beside me. She took my hand in hers.

"He's going to leave again," I said. The tears rolled down my face.

6

The Altar in the Bedroom

Baba didn't leave, but he grew ever more distant. He spent all day shut in his room or hiding behind Carola. I wanted to talk to him, but he didn't give me a chance. Whatever I said, the reply always came from Carola—until I couldn't stand it any more.

One day, when I came home from school, Baba was sitting stretched out in the armchair, as though dozing or deep in thought, with Carola resting on his chest. It was the first time since he'd been back that I had been able to take a good look at his face. It was a face that had known wind and frost, the hardships of life; a face troubled by grief. After all these years, he had still not got over losing Mama. A wave of pity passed through me.

"Baba," I called.

He didn't respond. I called again and stepped closer.

I was only a step away from him, when Carola suddenly

leapt up from Baba's chest, blocking my way.

"He's Carolo, not your baba."

Dumbstruck, I stared at Baba, his face now hidden behind Carola. Finally I drummed up courage. "Baba, there's something I want to talk to you about."

But, again, it was Carola who spoke. "His name is Carolo. He's not your baba, don't you understand?" The voice was shrill on my ear, like the jangling shells on her wrist.

Instinctively I took a step back, and tried to calm myself. "Baba, please, I really need to talk to you."

Carola lunged at me. "How many times do I have to tell you, his name is Carolo, he's not your baba," she snapped. "Go away. Just go away."

In a fit of anger, I pushed Carola aside. "Baba..."

"You are never to lay a finger on Carola again, do you understand? You are not to touch her!"

It was a face I had never seen before: distant and angry, and very serious. Baba never used to lose his temper with me in the past, no matter what I had done to upset him or how naughty I had been. His expression scared me.

"Go away. Go away. Tell her to go away," screeched Carola. Her shell bracelets jangled and screeched.

"Go," ordered Baba, "you're disturbing us."

I walked back to my room, numb as wood. A terrible notion was rising in my heart. *Baba doesn't love me any more.*

After that day, Baba did not say a single word to me, not even through Carola.

Nainai continued to focus her energy on her Buddhist sutras, and apart from Ah Fen calling the cat to eat, the house returned to its cold and desolate state.

I went back to the forest, but even there I could not be entirely myself.

I would often see Baba sitting by Mama's grave, and wonder what he was talking to her about. I was sure that if he were talking to her through Carola, she wouldn't be happy about it.

If Mama were still alive, she would hate the way Baba had changed.

In order to avoid meeting Baba in the forest, I would hang around at the edge of the marshes, where the grass grew waist high. As long as I didn't stand up, Baba wouldn't see me there. He seldom walked that way anyway. I couldn't run around, but I could lie back and watch the sky and the clouds drifting by, and think things over in peace. My duck friends would waddle over to see me, and dragonflies, toads and little insects would take me by surprise by landing on my body as I lay there.

But my mind couldn't settle. I no longer felt at peace. From my hiding place in the marshes, I kept glancing over at the forest. I longed to see Baba, and at the same time, hoped that I wouldn't. My thoughts were restless, unable to keep still, as though my entire being was constantly running up and down. To make matters worse, it was the rainy season and every afternoon there was a thunderstorm. I had to hurry home before the rain started to fall, or I'd be caught in it like a drowned chicken.

One afternoon, the sky went dark more suddenly than usual. Heavy black clouds threatened to break over the house. I was pleased with myself for having made it home before the downpour, but the moment I stepped through the door, there was a voice from the darkness.

"And where do you think you've been?"

I leapt out of my skin. In the dim light, I spotted Baba, sitting in the corner, holding Carola.

My heart was pounding. "Baba," I said quietly. I couldn't see his face, which was hidden behind Carola.

Carola's eyes were open wide. She looked as if she might gobble me up.

I shrank back and shot a glance at Nainai, who was sitting at the far end of the lounge, her blue jacket and trousers almost indistinguishable from the darkness. I couldn't see her expression, but I sensed she was angry. Perhaps I had interrupted another of her and Baba's rows.

"She's not a little girl any more. You should be here to keep an eye on her and provide her with guidance."

Nainai's voice was cold. I wasn't sure if this was for my benefit, or if she was reminding Baba of his responsibilities as a father.

"I want you to stop going to the forest," Baba said sternly, through Carola.

"But I go there to see Mama," I said meekly.

Nainai's response came out of the blue. "She's dead—you don't need to see her," she retorted angrily, then she got up and went upstairs.

I didn't know which way to turn. My eyes drifted to Baba, still hidden behind Carola.

"Shouldn't you be getting on with your homework?" Carola's shrill voice cut through the darkness.

I went to my room in silence. The storm had yet to break, but I was already drenched with sweat. My hands and feet were wet and slippery. My hair and my shirt were soaked and clinging to my back. The air was so close I could barely breathe. I had waited so many years, and this was the result. I couldn't accept it. I simply couldn't accept how things were.

But there was nothing I could do about it.

If Baba had brought home a real child, then I could fight—or negotiate. But I was facing a cloth doll, and I was powerless. I felt frustrated and desperate.

For the next few days, it kept threatening to rain rather than raining, and the air was so close I felt I was going mad. I stopped going to the forest, and did not dare to hang around in the garden. For some reason, I felt Carola was watching me. I stayed in my room, but still a sinister presence seemed to be closing in on me. Now and then I would glance behind me, as though she were sitting there watching me. I became so anxious I could barely answer the questions in my homework, let alone study anything new.

I stood by the window, gazing out at the clouds. As the sky grew darker, the clouds came so low they were almost touching the ground. But the rain still didn't fall. The air was so thick it was hard to breathe.

I started to paint, furiously covering the same sheet of paper over and over, till all the colours merged into one—black and foreboding, like the dark cloud weighing down in the sky. It was something I had to do. I needed to release the terror and anger inside me, or I would go mad.

"Ah…" There was a faint voice in Baba's room.

I jerked my head towards the sound, and my eyes went straight to the little door by the wardrobe.

"Why aren't we leaving? There's no point staying here." It was Carola.

Silence.

Sweat dripped on to my painting, one drop after another.

More silence.

The beads of sweat on the paper gradually spread. Each new drop landed with a splash that set the others trembling. I wanted to wipe them away, but my hands were shaking.

"I can't stand it here. Take me away!" The shell bracelets jangled as Carola spoke.

"We still have the performance. We can't leave before then." Baba's tone was weak and pained.

"Excuses, excuses! We can leave any time you want to. But you can't let go of her, can you?" Her voice was aggressive.

"Don't push me…" said Baba.

"She'll hurt you. The sooner you leave her, the better."

Another silence.

She? Carola couldn't have been talking about Nainai. She must have meant me.

I stared at the little door, my eyes as wide as they would go, my heart beating fast. The next thing I knew, I was by the door. It was shut tight. Even if it had been open, it would have been black as lacquer inside—I wouldn't have been able to see a thing. How I longed to open that door!

But I was also scared of upsetting Baba.

I forced myself to go back to my desk. I held my brush and spread more paint over the paper. But my heart was still by the door.

After a long pause, there was a murmur from Baba's room. I focussed my attention and listened to the low voice.

"Liur, Liur."

He was calling me. Baba was calling me! My heart leapt with excitement.

"Why are you saying her name? I won't have it!" Carola shouted, as shrill as ever.

"Liur, Liur…" Baba's voice was soft as silk on water, so faint it was barely audible.

When I came to my senses, I discovered that drops of rain were coming in through the open window, as though human hands had pierced the black clouds, and water was pouring out of the sky, fast and furious.

"Stop saying her name. I don't want to hear it again!" The urgency of the rain drowned out Carola's voice, but there was no mistaking her anger.

Baba ignored her. He continued to call for me. Without realising what I was doing, I stood up and followed his voice to the door. I pushed it open. It was black as lacquer inside, just as I'd expected.

I stood there like an idiot, and while I was dithering —should I go in, should I not go in—a flash of lightning split the sky, momentarily lighting up the room. Then it was over, and the room was in darkness again. My eyes were surrounded by blackness, and it seemed I could see my own heart beating furiously.

Baba's room was completely changed!

There was no bed, no wardrobe, not even a desk. The walls were a different colour. When had they become dark red?

Ah Fen's new curtains were gone, and the entire room was pitch black, but for the flickering of ghostly shadows.

Where the bed had been, there now stood a platform that looked very much like a sacrificial altar. There were two candles on it, one on each side, with a small saucer of red liquid between them. And beside the platform there was a row of stones.

I thought I must be mistaken. I waited until my eyes were used to the dark. But it was true. The ghostly atmosphere was more terrifying than anything I'd ever known.

"Liur…"

Baba called my name again, and somehow I found the courage to move. Taking a grip of my fear, I slowly shuffled forward, quietly answering his call. "Baba."

There was no response.

"Baba," I called again, but there was still no response.

The driving rain brought a cool freshness, but the thunder and lightning set my nerves on edge. Trembling with fear, I walked towards the altar, my legs shaking, my whole body on the brink of collapse.

I looked around me. Where were Baba and Carola?

When the next flash of lightning came, I saw Carola sitting on a stone beside the altar.

She hadn't been there before! When had she moved? Had I not seen clearly—or did she really have magic powers?

I was scared, but my curiosity drove me on. I summoned all my courage, and told myself: "It's only a ventriloquist's doll. Don't be scared."

But I couldn't stop shaking. I told myself not to be so stupid, not to be such a coward, but my legs refused to go any closer.

Then I heard Baba calling me again.

"Liur, Liur…"

The sound of his voice gave me courage, and I started to move. My heart was beating so hard it was almost leaping out of my chest.

When I was just a few steps from Carola, there was a crash of thunder and more lightning lit up the room. In that moment, I saw two blinding flashes shoot from Carola's eyes and I let out a scream. I stepped backwards, and in my panic, I tripped and fell.

The desire to flee rushed through me. Again I told myself, "It's only a ventriloquist's doll. If it weren't for Baba, it wouldn't be able to do anything at all."

As I was picking myself up from the floor, I heard Carola's provocative tone again: "Carolo is mine. You keep your distance from him. Do you understand?"

"That's not true! He's my baba," I answered, with a courage I did not know I had.

Carola laughed coldly. "Really? So why does he ignore you?"

"Be-cause..." I stuttered. I was unable to find a reason.

"Because his heart died a long time ago—when your mama died. Now he's like me, a person without a soul. He can never love you again. He's my Carolo, not your baba. Now do you understand?" Her tone made my hair stand on end.

"That's nonsense. He was calling me just now," I shouted angrily.

"That was the drink talking." She gestured with her hand, and I saw Baba curled up in the corner. His face was so pale he looked like a corpse.

"What happened?" I asked in a panic.

"I just told you, didn't I? He's drunk. He's out of his mind. He's always been like this," said Carola.

"Baba!" I ran over to him.

"Go away!" Baba waved his arms about. His breath reeked of alcohol.

"Baba, it's me, Liur. Look at me!" I grabbed his hand.

"Don't talk to him. He's drunk. Like a corpse."

"It must be you..." I glanced back in anger—then froze to the spot. Carola was no longer on the altar. She was standing right behind me.

I panicked. "Baba, wake up! Baba!" I called, shaking him. But he was like a sack of wet clay. I couldn't move him.

"Carolo, wake up! Tell this annoying child to go away."

Baba opened his eyes and stared at me for a long moment, as though not recognising me.

"Baba, it's me, Liur. Get up—let's go into the other room."

"Tell her to go away." Carola's voice was sharp and shrill.

Baba screwed up his eyes as he looked at me. Eventually he recognised me. "Liur..." he said weakly.

"Baba, get up. I'll help you." I grabbed his hand.

"Go..." said Baba. There was no strength in his voice.

"Baba, let's go."

"Carolo, I don't like her. Tell her to go away." Carola's voice gave me goosepimples.

"Baba, get up. Come on, get up!" I pulled his arms, but he showed no interest in moving. He closed his eyes and looked pained.

"Come on! Tell her to go away! Didn't you hear me?" Carola was insistent.

"Baba..." I summoned all my strength and tried to

yank him to his feet, but he pushed me aside.

"Go away." Baba's voice was flat. He was powerless.

"Baba!" I moved closer to him.

"Go away!" This time his voice was louder and full of pain.

Furious, I turned to face Carola—but she was the first to speak.

"Perhaps now you'll believe me. Everyone thinks I'm just a ventriloquist's doll, dependent on Carolo. The truth is, he is dependent on me. Without me, he's a useless drunk. Without me, he could never have become a ventriloquist."

Her words shocked me. I glanced at Baba. He was leaning against the wall, his head back, staring upwards with that same pained look he had when Mama died.

"He's always been like this. When your mama died, his heart died too. There are only two things in this world that help him forget his pain: one is alcohol; the other is me. Sometimes, even I cannot help him."

I wanted to argue with her, but seeing Baba's pain and sorrow, I could not find the words. I just stood there like an idiot, staring at her.

"Go away. Your being here upsets him."

"I want to take him out of this room," I persisted.

"Carolo, tell her to go away!" Carola roared once more.

Baba opened his eyes, looked at me, and then, waving

his hand, said, "Go away!"

"Baba…" Tears fell as I called his name.

"Go away! Go away!" he said. Then he raised his voice. "GO AWAY! GO AWAY!"

I got up and walked to the door.

"Close the door behind you," came Carola's voice.

I glanced back as I reached for the handle, and was shocked by what I saw.

Carola had wriggled her way into Baba's arms. Baba was stroking her back tenderly, and muttering, "My girl, my good little girl."

As the door clicked shut, my heart shattered.

7

Writing to Baba

"You mean Carola can move by herself?" It was clear from Qing Qing's face that she couldn't believe what she'd just heard.

"It's true. Not only move, but also—" I suddenly froze.

"Liur, what's the matter?"

I had been so scared and so shocked in Baba's room that I hadn't paid attention to Carola's eyes. But as I was relating the scene to Qing Qing, those eyes, full of vengeance, started to float in front of me. My whole body was shaking. "Her eyes were so frightening; she was staring at me," I flustered.

"That's impossible. Her eyes are made from glass beads. You must have made a mistake."

"I didn't make a mistake. Honestly, they were staring at me. Qing Qing, she really has magic powers."

"That's impossible." Qing Qing was still not convinced.

"She said so herself—have you forgotten?"

"That was your baba acting as ventriloquist. He was teasing us. Surely you didn't believe it?"

"That's what I thought too. But yesterday Baba was so drunk that he couldn't speak without slurring his words. He couldn't have been a ventriloquist in that condition. Do you know what Carola said? She said Baba's act is a sham, and that every word she says comes out of her own mouth."

"Liur, the more you say, the crazier it sounds."

"Qing Qing, you have to believe me. You know I wouldn't lie."

"I know, it's just … how can a ventriloquist's doll have magic powers?"

"She's not an ordinary doll—she came from an old grave."

"So what? All that means is that she was buried in a grave for a few centuries. She's still a doll, just a ventriloquist's doll!"

"What do I have to say to make you believe me?" I snapped.

"Don't be upset, Liur." Qing Qing patted my arm and, with a smile, she took something out of her schoolbag.

"This is for you. My ma made it last night—it's the chestnut cake you like so much."

My face was still tense, and I didn't take the paper bag

with the cake in it.

"Go on, eat the cake and I'll help you think it through."

My eyes lit up. "Do you think you can help?"

"I don't know, but I'm willing to try. Go on, eat the cake!"

I had no idea what kind of answer Qing Qing might come up with, but her confident smile reassured me.

Qing Qing put her arm around me. "Come on, I want to show you something!" She led the way to the school noticeboard. It was covered with information about the Water God Festival, including an eye-catching poster, with enormous writing across the top:

ALL THE WAY FROM SOUTH AMERICA
CAROLO & CAROLA
VENTRILOQUIST ACT

And there was a photo of Baba holding Carola.

"Everyone's talking about it," said Qing Qing.

I stared at the photo. "I wish I were a ventriloquist's doll," I said with feeling.

"Why on earth would you want that? They can't talk, can't walk, can't do anything for themselves."

"I just want to be with Baba. I wouldn't care if I couldn't walk or talk. What difference would that make?"

"Listen to you… You poor little thing." Qing Qing put

her arm around me, as though comforting a small child. "Why don't you come home with me after school? My ma says she hasn't seen you for days. She misses you!"

That day after school, the sky was dark as usual. I stayed for a while at Qing Qing's house, then rushed home before the rain started. When I stepped inside the house, I heard Baba and Carola talking. They were rehearsing for the Water God Festival. I stood in the doorway, watching.

Baba didn't notice me. He looked thin and pale. His body was sinking into the back of the chair, his hand idly stroking her back. It was a gesture of love that filled me with envy.

"You have to respond! It's not as though I can perform by myself." Carola was criticising Baba.

"I'm tired—give me a break!" said Baba weakly.

"You're always drunk. No wonder you're so tired. From now on, there's to be no more drinking."

"OK."

"You say that every time. Have you ever kept your word?"

Baba answered with a sigh and squeezed his eyes shut, so tightly that his eyebrows were touching.

"Look at you… Trying to do the right thing, but getting everything wrong. You're hopeless," Carola scoffed.

"Does she know?" Baba's eyes were still closed, his voice soft as silk floating on water.

"She's seen it with her own eyes, clear as crystal, and is utterly disappointed in you."

"Have I said anything that hurt her?"

"You told her to go away, to stop bothering you."

Baba hung his head on his chest. "How could I do that to her? That was going too far…"

I wanted to run to him, to tell him that I didn't blame him—but I could see the menacing look in Carola's eyes. She seemed to know that I was watching them. Her gaze drifted over to the door, warning me to keep my distance.

This time, I saw it for real—Carola's eyes were full of hate. She loathed me.

Then the rain started, heavy drops beating down, fast and furious. When I glanced back to Baba and Carola, there was no one there. The room was empty. I stood in the doorway, as though I'd forgotten what I was doing. I listened to the rain crashing to the ground, so hard it could rouse the gods.

"I called you so many times. Why didn't you answer me?" Ah Fen had come looking for me. She pulled me inside. "The rain's coming in. Hurry up and close the door."

By then there was water all over the threshold and my school bag was wet through.

The next day at school, I was about to tell Qing Qing everything I'd seen, but she spoke first. "My ma says you're the only one who can help your ba now."

I looked at her blankly, and she continued:

"I told her about your ba's drinking."

"Does she believe that Carola has magic powers?"

"I didn't tell her, but she says your ba must be very lonely, to be leaning on Carola so much. And she said your ba can't carry on getting more and more depressed. You have to help him."

"Of course I want to help him. But if he won't talk to me what am I supposed to do?"

"Well, I've thought of a solution for you!" Qing Qing said with a smile. "You can write him a letter. I can't believe Carola would stop him reading a letter."

It was a very good idea.

That day I was miles away in class. All I could think about was writing to Baba. Qing Qing helped me, and before we left school that day, we had written a letter:

Baba,

Do you know how happy I am that you have come back? I have so many things that I want to tell you, but whenever I talk to you, you reply as a ventriloquist. At first, it was like the games of make-believe we used to play when I was little, but it's gone on too long, and it's not fun any more. Because it's not you I'm talking to, but a doll, and that's a very strange feeling. Maybe you are used to speaking as a ventriloquist, but I don't like it when Carola speaks in your place. I want to talk to you face to face. I can't sit on your lap and chatter away like I used to when I was little, but I still want to look at you. Do you remember how you used to tell me that when you talk to someone you should look into their eyes if you want to have a meaningful conversation? I didn't understand back then, but now I can experience that feeling for myself. So, Baba, please could you put Carola to one side, so we can talk properly?

That day you told me to go away, I wasn't angry, but I was very worried for you. You looked so hurt. I wanted to comfort you, but I didn't know how, and you didn't give me a chance. Have you any idea how worried I was?

Baba, I'd love to go on walks with you again, to do lots of things with you, just like we did before. And I'd love to hear your stories. Although I'm not a little girl any more, and don't need to be looked after all the time, I have such happy memories of the time we used to spend together. Baba, please will you spend more time with me?

Your daughter,

Liur

Was the letter good enough? I wasn't sure. I wanted to improve it, but I didn't know how. Qing Qing read it and said it was fine as it was, and that if I wrote any more it would sound soppy.

That made me feel better.

My plan was to put the letter in Baba's room, but when I got home, I found the little door had been sealed up.

The letter stayed in my schoolbag for two days, until I happened to be there when Ah Fen was bringing in the washing, so I quickly slipped it into the pocket of one of Baba's shirts.

Then there was the torment of waiting. I didn't know how Baba would react. I was on edge. I couldn't settle, and neither could Qing Qing. Several days passed, and there was still no response.

"Do you think he may not have read it?" Qing Qing asked.

I couldn't answer. I didn't want to consider that possibility. I decided to write again.

This time, I added: *Mama knows you have come back, and she must be so happy, but she'd be very upset if she knew you weren't talking to me properly.*

And I wrote a few things that I'd heard at Qing Qing's house: *Auntie says you are avoiding me because I look so much like Mama, and that it must be painful for you. I can understand that, but don't you think it's unfair on me?*

When Mama died, I hurt just like you. When you left, I was all alone. You're back now, but you're more distant than ever.

This time, I saw Baba with my own eyes, reading the letter.

I had put it on Mama's grave, then hidden to one side and waited. Baba didn't show up that day and the letter got soaked in the rain. But I wasn't discouraged. I went home, copied it out again and put it on Mama's grave the next day. I waited three days in a row, and finally got the result I wanted.

From my hiding place, I watched Baba pick up the letter, read it and cry. I couldn't stop myself: I went over to him, stood silently behind him, and then finally I called his name.

He hadn't expected me. He was flustered. He panicked and ran off. Was he scared of me seeing his weaker side, or was he angry with me? I felt so stupid. I hadn't expected him to react like this. I called out to him and watched as he disappeared into the forest.

As the afternoon rain poured from the sky, tears gushed from my eyes.

I threw myself on Mama's grave. "Did I do something wrong? Mama, please tell me what I've done wrong?" I asked over and over. "Why won't Baba have anything to do with me? Doesn't he love me any more?"

Mama didn't respond in her usual way. Instead of answering my call with a softly murmuring breeze, the air was completely still. There were only the raindrops beating on her gravestone, whipping my heart.

"Mama, are you ignoring me now too?" I wanted to ask, but no sound would come out. Two lines of hot tears ran down my face.

8

Moonlight Ritual

When I came back from the forest, I fell ill. My body was burning and I was aching all over. I felt so confused. I longed for a good sleep, but the faint voices that carried through from Baba's room were loud enough to prevent me from falling asleep. I couldn't make out what they were saying, but I could feel the tension in the atmosphere.

That night my throat was unbearably dry. I was just about to get up for a drink of water, when I noticed Carola sitting at the foot of the bed, looking at me severely. I broke out in a cold sweat. Hastily I glanced around the room for Baba, but he wasn't there.

I was scared, but the thought that Baba had been in to see me warmed my heart. I glanced at Carola. Her stern, grave eyes made me shiver. I wanted to overcome my cowardice, and quietly called Baba's name. I wanted to apologise to him, to tell him that I would never do anything to hurt him ever again. I waited and waited, but Baba didn't appear. Where on earth was he? Why would he leave Carola in my room?

She was still staring at me. I looked down, not daring to look her in the eye. I could hear my heart beating faster and faster, as though it were going to burst out of my chest. *Baba, Baba, come quickly!* I felt like I was suffocating. But I couldn't help raising my head to stare at Carola. She smiled at me coldly, then turned around and walked slowly towards the little door to Baba's room.

When I realised she was moving by herself, I screamed.

Ah Fen came running. "What's the matter?" she asked.

I stuttered and stammered, and managed to get a few sounds out—but putting them together in coherent sentences was beyond me.

"Another nightmare?" asked Ah Fen, as she wiped the sweat from my brow. "At least your temperature's going down."

That evening, I clung so tightly to Ah Fen that she couldn't leave until I was asleep.

Ah Fen said I'd had a nightmare. I wished it had been a nightmare, but it wasn't. Carola really had been in my room. She had been sitting on my bed.

"If things carry on like this, I'm going to go mad," I told Qing Qing when she came to see me the following afternoon.

"Are you absolutely certain it wasn't a dream?" Qing Qing still didn't believe that Carola had magic powers.

"I saw it as clear as day. If you don't believe me, forget it." I was getting impatient.

"Liur, it's not that I don't believe you, it's just that…" Qing Qing got up and walked over to the little door by the wardrobe. "This door has been sealed up. How could Carola have gone from your room into your ba's?"

I was momentarily stumped for words, then blurted out, "She's not an ordinary doll—she's got magic powers."

I truly believed it—and the conviction made me even more anxious, even more on edge.

The following night, my temperature flared up again, like a fire raging inside me. Ah Fen gave me some antipyretic medicine to bring my fever down, and brought me an icepack to soothe my discomfort. I tossed and turned, before finally settling. I had just managed to fall asleep, when I was woken by a wild caterwauling.

At first I tried to ignore it, but the noise became more frenzied and urgent, as though some kind of riot was going on outside, so I got up and crept over to the window.

The scene before me was beautiful. There was a creamy

halo around the moon, which bathed the distant hills in subtle mystery, their contours suggesting a sleeping person. The caterwauling had subsided, but there was no sign of a cat. In the garden, all I could see were trees, silvered by moonlight.

I returned to bed, but couldn't get back to sleep. I stared at the ceiling, my heart filled with sadness.

Suddenly the screech of a cat tore through the quiet of night. High-pitched and menacing, it dragged me to my feet again. I stood by the window and traced the dark trees lining the path through the forest. In the faint moonlight, the path was empty and dark, until I came to the black shadow looming over it. It was Hu Niu, our feisty ginger tabby, her back arched ready to fight, her claws glistening in the moonlight, her cautious movements indicating that the enemy was nearby. There were wild cats in the forest, but they never came near the house and had a neither-friend-nor-foe relationship with Hu Niu and our black cat Ling Ling. So why had war suddenly broken out?

I was still pondering this, when I saw Hu Niu leap into the air, kicking off a huge commotion. Shadows flew in from all corners of the dark forest. Within moments, there were hordes of cats fighting and struggling, screeching and hissing.

I was alarmed by what I saw. Then I noticed that Hu

Niu and the wild cats had stopped fighting, and were surrounding something, ready to attack. At first, I couldn't see what it was, and when I realised, I cried out in shock.

It was Carola! The cats were surrounding Carola!

I couldn't believe my eyes. Was I dreaming? I bit my finger to check and felt the pain shoot though my body.

My eyes returned to the battle scene. I saw claws flying. The wild cats moved fast, but Carola fought deftly, her soft body dodging every attack. The shell bracelets jangled as she moved, and in the quiet of the night they sounded shriller even than the cats' cries.

One cat let out a desperate scream as she flew at Carola, baring her sharp claws. But Carola spun round. She had a flute in her hand and struck the cat's rear leg with it, knocking her to the ground.

The cats began to draw back. Ling Ling, our black cat, was about to leap away too, when she felt Carola's flute hard on the back of her leg. She let out a wail and fell to the ground. Hu Niu, still in fighting mode, hurled herself recklessly at Carola. But Carola was quick and agile, dodging her attacks, and retaliating faster than lightning. Even our ginger tabby wasn't a match for Carola, and she too let out a cry as she fell to the ground.

The other cats had retreated to the edge of the forest, and Carola did not pursue them. She stayed on the moonlit path, playing her flute. The flute music played on and on. Accompanied by the light tinkling of the shell bracelets, it had the effect of a lullaby. Gradually, the cats lay down on the ground. They looked as though they would never move again.

Carola turned around and faced the edge of the forest. That's when I noticed someone else in the shadows of the trees. Someone tall and thin, whom I recognised immediately.

Baba too played the flute as he walked towards Carola. He played the simplest tune, but it was haunting and arresting. He walked past Carola towards the cats. She followed him, circled the cats three times and started to dance. As the music sped up, Carola became became looser and freer, and the more she danced the more animated she became. When she raised her head, her lips looked red and freshly painted, and glinted in the moonlight in the most enchanting way.

As the flute music grew louder, Carola's dancing gained still more pace. She spun around and around, free and full of rhythm, as though she were a real child.

Then, as the flute music slowed, Carola's dancing slowed too. Baba whistled, and the cats on the ground woke and formed an orderly line. Hu Niu was at the front, Ling Ling was second. The cats had lost all their fighting force and were docile as sheep.

Carola jumped on to Hu Niu's back and glanced over her shoulder at Baba. He moved quickly to the front of the line and, like an elegant general, played the flute as he led his night troops on a full-moon march. Like a host of black shadows, neither human nor ghost, they floated effortlessly through the night like wandering souls. Not a speck of dust stirred beneath their feet.

As they came closer, the flute became faster, and the cats moved silently forward, rays of light shooting from their eyes, glinting like tiny fire-spirits. They walked up the forest path into the garden, and I stepped back from the window, crouching down out of sight.

When the sound of the flute moved away again, I dared to look out of the window. My eyes were drawn to Baba at the front of the line, playing the flute. Carola was sitting on Hu Niu's back and following closely behind were the cats, moving in time to the music, like sedated foot soldiers. They were heading deep into the forest.

After a while, the path disappeared into silent darkness.

I leaned against the wall, my body numbed as though hit by lightning. Terror gripped my mind. I had no other feelings.

9

The Punishment

The following morning, I felt ill all over again.

I forced myself to get out of bed. As I looked out of the window, I saw Ah Fen walking towards Hu Niu. The cat greeted her like the enemy at the gates, arching her back and growling deep in her throat. Her aggression shocked me.

"I don't know what's got into those cats," Ah Fen grumbled as she brought me my breakfast. "It was like they were spooked last night, they made such a racket."

"Did you hear it?" I asked quickly.

"I don't think anyone could've slept through the noise they were making."

"And did you see it?" My heart was racing.

"Oh, I didn't want to get up. But if they do it again, I'll have someone come and take them away."

"Ah Fen, it's that ventriloquist's doll—Baba's doll. It

was showing its power over the cats. It's magic—and it's a monster."

"What, more of this nonsense?" Ah Fen felt my forehead.

My temperature had gone down.

"Drink your milk, take your medicine, have a good sleep and tomorrow you can go back to school."

"Ah Fen, I saw it! It was terrifying. Carola—"

She didn't let me finish. "Drink your milk!"

"Ah Fen, I saw it! Honestly!"

"I haven't got time to listen to you rabbiting on about this stuff. Now, hurry up and take your medicine."

I did as I was told. I took the medicine and lay down. I waited until Ah Fen had gone, then got up again. I stood by the window, trying to spot some trace of what had happened in the night.

But there was no trace of blood in the garden, no sign of fighting. I watched Ling Ling leap over the fence and dart into the woods; there was no sign at all that she'd been injured. Was it possible that my illness had made me light-headed? Had I imagined it all?

"What's the matter with you? You look miles away." Qing Qing had come to see me again that afternoon. She looked concerned. "There's no colour in your lips. Are you all right?" She took my hand. "Oh, you're as cold as ice. Would you like my ba to come and see you?"

I shook my head and stared at her. I knew there was terror in my eyes.

"What's wrong?"

"If I tell you, you won't believe me!" I pulled my hand back.

"Is it Carola again?" Qing Qing bit her lip. "Go on, tell me. I'll believe you."

"Really?"

"Mm-hm." Qing Qing nodded.

"She's terrifying. . She drinks cat's blood…" I told her what I had seen in the night.

"Are you sure you weren't—" Qing Qing shot me a glance and swallowed the words that were on her lips.

"I knew you wouldn't believe me."

"It's not that I don't believe you." Qing Qing defended herself. "It's just that if the cat screamed so loudly, then Ah Fen and Nainai would have heard it too."

"Ah Fen did hear it. And she said it was horrible."

"And did she see your baba giving Carola cat's blood to drink?"

"She didn't get out of bed."

Qing Qing went quiet. I knew she didn't believe a word I'd said.

"Qing Qing, I've got a premonition she's going to hurt me."

"I don't believe a ventriloquist's doll can harm you."

Qing Qing put her arm around me. "But, don't worry, if she tries anything, I'll be merciless with her."

Qing Qing made me feel warm and comforted, but she wouldn't be able to protect me. As long as Carola was around, my life was in danger.

A few days later, the evening air was heavy with rain that wouldn't fall, the sky was an ominous colour of fire, and the old tree in the garden was groaning in the dusk. I stood by the window, overcome with a sense of loss.

Then I heard Qing Qing shouting at the front door. "Liur, come quickly, your nainai's had a fall!"

I dropped the book I was reading and ran outside. Qing Qing was alone and her voice was getting more and more urgent.

Baba came out, looking worried. "Where is she? Is she OK?" he asked her.

"She's at my house. My ma says the situation is dangerous, and I should come and tell you." I could hear the panic in her voice.

Baba ran straight over to Qing Qing's house. I wanted to go with him, but Qing Qing blocked my way. "Where's Carola?" she asked.

That's when I realised what Qing Qing had in mind.

I led her to Baba's room. There was something insidious about that room. I didn't dare turn on the light. Instead

I walked towards Carola in the gloom. She was sitting on the platform that looked like an altar, with her eyes closed as though sleeping.

I was about to step closer, when Qing Qing held me back.

"Let's agree something first—if Carola is just a cloth doll, then we'll leave immediately."

I nodded, then carefully, cautiously, went forward. Qing Qing was right beside me, her eyes fixed on the doll.

Even in the half light, we could see Carola's face clearly, her eyes closed as if in a sweet dream. Although it was a child's face, there was no concealing the traces of time. When I glanced at her closed mouth, I was surprised to find that her bright red lips had become so dark.

Carola looked no different from any other cloth doll, sitting there without any human senses. But foresight told me it was a pretence. *Don't be deceived*, I told myself silently.

Qing Qing reached out her hand and touched Carola. Instantly, her body slumped to one side. "Look, it's just a cloth doll!" she said.

I didn't make a sound, but an idea was forming in my mind. Whether or not she had magic powers, I had to take this opportunity to get rid of her. There was a hole in the ground near an old tree in the forest. I would take her there, throw her in the hole, and cover it with a big stone.

Qing Qing and I were the only ones who knew about the hole. Baba hadn't been back long, and he wouldn't know about it.

I stared at Carola, her eyes still closed as though unaware of her impending doom. She was taller and bigger than I remembered. I didn't know whether I'd be able to carry her, but I didn't care. I bent over and grabbed her.

"What are you doing?" Qing Qing blocked my way.

"I have to get rid of her."

"She's just a doll!" said Qing Qing.

"I don't care what she is—I have to get rid of her."

"But we agreed we'd only do something if she had magic powers. You can't go back on your word now."

Carola hadn't moved, but still I had an uneasy feeling.

"She's just an ordinary cloth doll. Let's go."

"Even if she is an ordinary cloth doll, I can't let her stay here!"

"If you get rid of her, your baba will be so angry and so hurt."

Qing Qing had found my weak spot. I would rather hurt myself than upset my baba. Images of him at the time of Mama's death floated in front of me. I closed my eyes in pain, and felt my whole body go limp.

"Liur, let's go! Your ba will be back soon."

Qing Qing had succeeded; I gave in.

But, as I turned to leave the room, I saw Carola open her eyes. Anger surged inside me, and I grabbed her again, hurled her to the ground and stamped on her like a lunatic.

Qing Qing seized hold of me, horrified. "Liur!" she shouted. "What are you doing?"

"She might fool you, but she doesn't fool me. She's evil and I can't let her stay here."

There was no reasoning with me. In my rage, I carried on kicking and stamping.

"Liur, stop it. Stop kicking…"

But I was entirely caught up in my madness. I stamped hard and kicked hard. I wanted to stamp her till she came apart. I didn't stop until a strong force gripped my arm, and someone pulled me back.

I hadn't seen Baba come in.

His face was black as iron; his eyes looked as though they were about to pop out of his head. I was so scared. My entire body was trembling.

Qing Qing stood to one side, her face ashen with fear. And behind Baba there was Nainai, who looked even more shocked.

Baba held Carola to his chest. Then he turned to Qing Qing and, suppressing his anger, said coldly, "I thought you were such a good girl. It never occurred to me that you might be deceitful. From now on, you're never to come to our home."

Qing Qing glanced at me in horror, then ran from the room.

The burning rage in Baba's eyes stunned me.

"Please leave us," Baba said gravely to Nainai. "I have to talk to Liur."

Nainai glanced at me and, without a word, she left the room.

As soon as Nainai had gone, Carola's voice started up. "Carolo, this child is so bad, she almost trampled me to death. You *must* teach her a lesson."

I knew I was no match for Carola. I looked meekly at Baba, whose face was still full of anger.

Carola's voice sounded again. "If you don't punish her, then never talk to me again."

Baba stroked Carola's head lovingly. "So how do you suggest we punish her?"

There was a flash of hatred in her eyes. "Forbid her to play in the garden, and forbid her to go to that girl's house."

I looked imploringly at Baba, but he turned away.

Carola continued, "And she is NOT to go to the forest. She is NOT to go and see her mama. You said this before, but you have let her get away with it."

The rage bubbling inside me started to boil over, and the words came bursting out. "I will go and play in the forest. I will go and see Mama. You can't stop me."

"Really? If you want to know how far I can go, just ask your father."

"Baba." My voice caught in my throat and I pleaded with him with my eyes.

Eventually, he spoke. "You heard what Carola said."

"Baba, do you really prefer that cloth doll to me?" Tears rolled down my face.

"Carolo, tell her to get out. I don't want to see that tiresome child a moment longer." Carola was moving impatiently from side to side, her shell bracelets jangling and scraping, with that same shrill, grating sound.

"Go!" Baba said coldly.

"If you don't let me go and see Mama, she will be so hurt." Holding back my tears, I added, "What will you tell her? That you would rather have a cloth doll than your own daughter? Would you dare say that to her?"

"GET OUT!" Baba roared.

The door opened and I saw Nainai's shocked face appear.

"GET OUT, ALL OF YOU!"

"If I'm such a nuisance, why did you come back?" I shouted at him. My face was wet with tears as I ran off.

From that day on, I was a prisoner. Apart from going to school, I was not allowed out.

The worst thing was that Qing Qing blamed me for

not keeping our agreement, and wouldn't talk to me any more.

I became the loneliest, most isolated person in the world.

10

The Water God Festival

On the day of the Water God Festival, I was astonished when Nainai asked Ah Fen to take me to see Baba's performance. I hadn't left the house for weeks, except to go to school.

Amid all the activity, in the sea of people, I bumped into Qing Qing and her family.

Uncle Ming De looked shocked when he saw me. "You're so thin!" he said. "And so pale. Have you been ill?"

I shook my head shyly.

"Is Nainai here?" he asked.

I shook my head again. Nainai was still angry that Baba wouldn't go back to the hospital.

Auntie came over. "Liur, we haven't seen you for such a long time," she said kindly. "Why don't you come to our house any more?"

"I'm not—" I didn't finish the sentence as Qing Qing was staring right at me.

Suddenly a man cut into our group and greeted Uncle Ming De enthusiastically. Immediately they got chatting, and Auntie joined their conversation too. I looked at Qing Qing. She was still angry. I didn't know if she'd ever be friends with me again.

I turned away sadly. Ah Fen had been swallowed up by the crowd, so I walked to the edge of the crowd and sat down under a tree on my own, watching the hordes of people coming and going.

The annual Water God Festival was one of the most important in our town. Like all the other children in town, I was told of its origins as soon as I was old enough to listen.

Three hundred years ago, when there were only a few families living in the town, everyone fetched their water from a single well. One year there was a drought, and the well dried up. The villagers all said the Water Gods had abandoned them. One by one, they moved away, until there was only one family left. Illness and old age had prevented this family from moving, and they depended entirely on one young boy. Every day this boy went out looking for food and water. At first, he could still find wild fruit, and bring water back from the marshy lowland. But gradually, the marshes dried up, and the plants withered and died. The thought of his sick parents and his elderly grandfather dying of thirst was too much for the boy, and he lay on the ground and started to cry. He cried and cried, and every one of his tears seeped into the earth. The boy cried until his tears ran dry, and he lost consciousness and collapsed.

As the night breeze blew over his face, the boy shivered and opened his eyes. He discovered that his body was soaked, and that there was water flowing by his feet. He leapt up in surprise, and in the light of the moon saw, just a few steps away from him, a spring of fresh water. He threw himself to the ground, put his mouth to the water and started to gulp. It was sweet as honey. He thought he must be dreaming, and knew that he must drink as much as he could in this dream. He drank and drank, until his belly was swollen. He looked at the spring, then looked all around him. It didn't seem like a dream.

Remembering his family, he filled a bag with water and ran home as fast as he could to tell them the good news. His grandfather was moved, said it must be a blessing from the Water God. He asked his grandson to help him walk to the spring, where he went down on his knees and touched his head to the ground over and over again, repeating humbly, "Thank you, Water God, for this gift of water."

The villagers who had moved away heard the news, and one after another, gradually came back to their homes. They built a pool beside the spring, and every year they held a celebration. Time passed and even though all the houses were now connected to the water supply, and the village had become a thriving town, the Water God Festival remained an important annual event.

This year would be like any other. There would be a thanksgiving ritual, followed by a programme of entertainments. Baba's ventriloquist act was the focus of everyone's attention. I heard people talking about it, and discussing the strange tale of how Baba had become a ventriloquist.

Suddenly there was a flurry of activity at the front of the crowd and, over the loudspeaker, I heard the host introduce Baba. All eyes turned to the stage. From my place at the back, I watched as Baba emerged from behind the curtain, holding Carola. He was wearing a smart suit, his hair was slicked back, and there was a big smile on his face. How different he was from the drunk curled up in the corner of the room at home. Carola looked full of life too. Her lips were red and shiny, as though she was wearing lipstick, and her eyes were bright: two shiny beads, gleaming in the light.

When Carola opened her mouth and greeted everyone, the audience burst into applause. I heard children

THE WATER GOD FESTIVAL

asking, "Can the doll really talk?" Even the adults were enthralled.

Once the introductions were over, Carola's body suddenly started to shake and there was a look of panic on her face.

The performance had begun.

Carolo: You look scared, Carola. What's the matter?

Carola: How could you do this to me? You know very well that of all the festivals, the one I fear the most is the Water God Festival. Yet you still brought me here. I'm leaving—by myself, if I have to. Goodbye.

Carolo: Wait! Wait! You're a cloth doll; how can you walk home by yourself?

Carola: I am not a cloth doll! If I was, how would I be able to talk?

Carolo: You can talk because…

Carola: Here you go again! Saying that I can only talk because of you!

She took a big step forward, faced the audience and raised her voice.

Carola: Friends, as you can see, his mouth does not move at all. So how can he be speaking for me? You know what they say: you can't play two flutes at the same time!

Carola placed her hands on her hips and raised her head. Her angry stance had the audience laughing out loud.

Carolo: Don't get so worked up. If I've said something wrong, I'm sorry.

Carola: That's more like it.

Carolo: You still haven't told everyone why you are so afraid of the Water God Festival?

Carola: Perhaps it's better if I don't tell them, in case I scare the children.

Carolo: But they want to know!

Carola: I'm not telling.

Carolo: Friends, would you like to know?

"YES!" shouted the audience. And the children standing closest to the stage shouted excitedly, "We're not scared! Tell us! Tell us!"

Carolo: Now, you have to tell them!

Carola: All right then, I'll tell them. But when I've finished, they'll have to run away fast!

Carolo: Hey, why are you talking like this! If the audience runs away, then who will we be performing for?

Carola: I'm only thinking of the children!

Carolo: Don't worry—what you're afraid of can't happen here.

Carola: You adults are all the same, tricking the children with your lies. I didn't believe it myself until my best friends started disappearing one by one. And then I stopped believing what adults say.

Carolo: What happened?

Carola: One day, my good friend, Umata, came looking for me. She told me that she was going travelling, and that her parents had made her a set of lovely new clothes. I thought it was very strange—her family was poor; how could they have money to send her travelling and make new clothes for her? So I followed her secretly, and do you know what I discovered?

Carolo: What?

Carola: I saw her baba giving her something to drink. Then she fell asleep. Her mama started to cry. Her baba said, "Umata is so pretty—the Water God is sure to love her." And then they—

The audience was wide-eyed, waiting for Carola to continue. Carolo urged her to speak on.

Carolo: What did they do to her? Tell us!

Carola: They… Oh, it's very scary. It's better that I

don't say.

The audience was getting restless. "Tell us, tell us!"

> **Carola:** They took Umata to a stream. People gathered around her, and the priest was there too.

Carola paused and asked the audience, "Are you really not scared?"

The audience shouted, "WE'RE NOT SCARED!"

> **Carolo:** They say they're not scared. Tell them!
> **Carola:** Should I really?
> **Carolo:** Yes, you must. Why did they take Umata to a stream?
> **Carola:** They were praying for rain. When the ritual was over, they took Umata—
> **Carolo:** And what did they do?
> **Carola:** They dropped her over the edge of the cliff into the valley below.

The crowd gasped.

> **Carola:** I've finished now. Why aren't you all running away?
> **Carolo:** Things like that may have happened back in

your day, but they can't happen now.

Carola: Back in my day? Aren't we living in the same era?

Carolo: We're living in the same era now—but you are so much older than us.

Carola: That's right—if you hadn't mentioned it, I would have forgotten.

Carolo: Friends, do you know how old Carola is?

Carola: You're going too far now. You can't talk about a girl's age in public! I'm going to ignore you.

Carola put her hands on her hips, turned her head to one side and looked angry.

Carolo: OK, OK. I won't tell them. Let's talk about the Water God Festival instead!

Carola: It's not right. You have to apologise first.

Carolo: OK, OK. I apologise.

Carola: That's more like it. You told me these people aren't afraid of drought. If they're not afraid, why do they sacrifice to the Water God?

Carolo: The Water God sacrifice is just a ritual, to remind everyone to think about where their water comes from. Now that there's a reservoir, there shouldn't be any more droughts.

Carola: Is this true?

She turned to the audience. "YES!" they cried.

Carola: Then I don't need to worry any more. Carolo, let's go and take a look around the market!

Carolo: Wait a minute, you still haven't told the audience why droughts are so frequent where you come from?

Carola: It's because it seldom rains there. We drink melted snow from the Andes. But if the weather's too warm, the snow melts too fast. And if it doesn't snow enough in winter, then we'll be short of water.

Carolo: You come all the way from the Andes! What's it like there?

Carola: It's such a beautiful place. Our village lies at three thousand feet, high up where the mountains are white and the lakes are blue. The view is spectacular. It's like living in the clouds!

Carolo: Three thousand feet? Can you still breathe at that height?

Carola: Of course! And when our people start to sing it sounds incredible!

Carolo: Would you sing a song for us now?

Carola: Oh, no! There are too many people. I'd be embarrassed!

Carolo: Would you like to hear Carola sing, everyone?

"YES" the audience shouted back.

Carola waved her hand frantically in the air, her shell bracelets jangling.

> **Carola:** They're very insistent, aren't they? They really want to hear me sing.
> **Carolo:** You see, everyone is so enthusiastic. How can you not sing now!
> **Carola:** I'm touched! So to thank them for their wonderful welcome, I'll sing them a folksong from home.

And with that, Carola started to sing.

Her voice was as clear and bright as if it had come from a mountain valley. Although we couldn't understand the words, it was utterly enchanting. The audience was transfixed, and so was I. She swayed as she sang, in a beautiful and graceful dance. She could be a real, living girl. Why couldn't Qing Qing see that?

Then, all of a sudden, I remembered something—Baba couldn't sing! So how could he sing so beautifully as a ventriloquist? I stared at him, but all I could see was the smile on his face, and his body moving in time with Carola's. He didn't seem to be controlling her in the slightest. She appeared to be singing all by herself.

Carola sang several songs. Her voice was as polished as

the very best singers. Her gestures and body movements were constantly changing, and her performance, so full of emotion, had the audience wide eyed and gawping like fools or drunks.

When she finished singing, she thanked everyone profusely.

The audience adored her.

The host waited for the crowd to settle down again, and then asked the very question that was on my mind: "Mr Carolo, please tell us, how do you sing so well?"

Baba was about to open his mouth when Carola interrupted. "That's a very strange question to ask. Carolo hasn't sung a single word. How can you possibly know how he sings?"

The audience roared with laughter.

The host was full of praise. "Mr Carolo, what an astonishing achievement! Your performance was simply magical—"

Carola leapt about, yelling like a lunatic. "I was the performer, so why aren't you asking me?"

The host began to look unsure. "I thought this was a ventriloquist act. Am I mistaken?"

Carola glared at him indignantly. "A ventriloquist act? It was entirely my own performance. It had nothing to do with him."

There was a look of surprise on the host's face. "Really?"

he asked.

"If you don't believe me, why don't you ask him to sing?" Carola said smugly.

Carolo pretended to be angry. "You're determined to embarrass me, aren't you, Carola?"

Carola ignored him. "You see, he can't sing!" she told the host.

Now the host was intrigued. "Mr Carolo, how about a few lines, to let everyone know if the cloth doll is telling the truth or not?"

Carola was pushing him too. "Come on, Carolo, sing!"

Baba's face flushed red. He cleared his throat and started to sing. His notes were all over the place. He was completely out of tune. Every time his voice caught in his throat, the audience winced, and the host made a show of covering his ears. I could feel the emotion rising inside me, because this was the Baba I remembered.

When Baba stopped singing, he stood there looking self-conscious. "Well, you did ask me," he said, defensively.

The audience gave him an enthusiastic round of applause. "Remarkable! Astonishing!" exclaimed the host.

Carola turned to the host, striking an angry pose. "What's wrong with you? His singing was terrible. Why do you praise him?"

The host smiled at her. "I'm sorry, Miss Carola, I got

carried away. Please forgive me. May I invite you to sing another song for us?

Carola struck another pose. "Singing a few songs is no problem, but this time you need to be clear that he is himself and I am myself, and that when I perform it has nothing to do with him."

The host smiled. "Yes, yes, yes. You are a remarkable singer, Miss Carola. Please go ahead, we're all ears."

So Carola sang again, earning yet more applause from the audience.

But while the audience was caught up in Carola's performance, I had been distracted by a conversation nearby.

"Everyone says that if the old doctor had operated, and not Kai Xiang, then his wife might still be alive."

"Kai Xiang's not cut out to be a doctor. It took him ten years of medical school to qualify. If it weren't for the family having its own hospital, he'd never had made it in the profession."

"I heard it was the old doctor who made him do the surgery. He never imagined that Kai Xiang would kill his own wife. And then he made him leave."

"But he couldn't have stayed, could he? If you murder someone, you have to face the law…"

"It's more likely to have been a case of professional negligence."

"He'd still be liable if it were professional negligence. No wonder he didn't dare come back sooner..."

I focused my attention on the small group of speakers, and recognised one of them as a cleaner from the hospital. I didn't know if what they were saying was true or not, but it shocked me all the same. Had Baba really been responsible for Mama's death? No, I couldn't believe it. Yeye had said the outcome would have been the same no matter who had done the operation. But if Baba hadn't made an error, would he still have been so depressed? And they'd said he couldn't return to the hospital, wasn't fit to be a doctor any more. Could it be that he'd run away not only from grief, but also from guilt?

I kept my eyes on the group while I thought it over. They seemed to have a lot to say.

"The important thing is not whether something went wrong during the operation. He's a doctor and he didn't even know that his wife was ill. How crazy is that?"

"Yes, that *was* strange. When someone's ill, there are always symptoms. Even if he hadn't spotted them himself, surely someone in the family would have noticed something?"

The last sentence hit me like a hammer on the head. I knew Mama had fainted, but I hadn't said anything. That would make me responsible for her death as well, wouldn't it? She hadn't wanted me to tell Baba—even when she fainted a second and a third time, I still pretended nothing had happened. How could I have been so naïve?

But it wasn't naïvety. I had been scared that her illness would steal Baba's attention from me... Oh god, how could I have been so evil! I looked at Baba on the stage and was filled with remorse. My eyes began to blur with tears.

11

Child-Souls in the Mountains

Not long after the Water God Festival, the school broke up for the summer holidays.

In the past, I couldn't have been happier when the holidays started, but this time I was grumpy and miserable. This time, the holidays meant I'd have to stay at home every day, and live under constant torment from Carola.

On the last day of term, Qing Qing walked with me to fork in the road. She paused and said, "See you next term then, Liur."

I looked at her with a heavy heart and she added with deliberate lightness, "Next term, I'll tell you everything I did over the holidays—and you can tell me everything you did."

I held her hand, too sad to say anything, and now Qing Qing looked sad too. "Don't be like this—two months will pass very quickly."

"Qing Qing, I'm scared I'll never see you again."

"What is it this time?" she sighed.

"Whether you believe it or not, I've got a premonition that Carola is not going to leave me alone."

"Here you go again. She's just a ventriloquist's doll." Qing Qing looked impatient.

"She's not. Every evening she—Oh, forget it. If I told you, you wouldn't believe me." I swallowed the words I was going to say, turned and walked away.

"Liur, don't drive yourself further into a corner." Qing Qing ran after me, but I didn't respond. Instead I sped up and started to run.

I heard Qing Qing call after me, but I didn't look back. In my heart I was saying, "Goodbye, Qing Qing."

From the first day of the summer holidays, I felt like I was suffocating.

After his success at the Water God Festival, so many people invited Baba to go and perform for them that I never knew whether he'd gone out or was in his room drunk again. A few times I had heard Carola having a go at him, arguing that it was time to leave. But I didn't hear Baba's voice. Nainai's room was equally quiet, and even Ah Fen moved about like a phantom, her footsteps inaudible. The whole house was like a ghost town, the atmosphere so oppressive that you couldn't breathe.

There was a pile of books on my desk, but my heart wasn't in them. Most of the time I felt groggy and just wanted to sleep.

One day, I was standing by the window, looking out at the garden. It was so empty—even the two cats had run off. There wasn't a cloud in the sky, just the sun blazing down. It almost was too bright to open my eyes.

I was bored out of my mind, staring at Mama's photograph.

Was this how Mama felt after the miscarriage?

Suddenly, a thought came into my head: could it be that Carola had come to get revenge for Mama?

It was a terrifying thought, but a ridiculous one—I quickly rejected it. Mama loved me so much; she could never do something like that to me. She'd once said that Baba and I were the two people she loved most in the world, and that she'd do anything to make us happy. On more than one occasion, she had asked me to look after Baba, to keep him company. At the time, I hadn't understood why she was saying these things. Now I guessed that she must have known that she was seriously ill, and that was why she said them. As I looked at her photo, there was pain in my heart and I felt full of guilt.

During the day, my mind would wander, but as evenings drew in, a feeling of terror grew inside me. More than once, I had been woken in the night by Carola. She would sneak into my room, sit on my bed, with her eyes wide open, and stare at me. She didn't do anything, but if she had moved any closer, I wouldn't have been able to breathe. I'd scream at the top of my voice every time I woke to see those shining glass eyes staring at me. At first Ah Fen came running, but after it had happened a few times, she began to ignore me. Carola was so clever: scaring me, but making the others think I was having nightmares.

This went on for over a week and I couldn't stand it any longer. One day, when I saw Ah Fen was going shopping, I seized my opportunity and asked, "Could you take to the library on your way, and pick me up on your way back?"

Ah Fen looked uncomfortable.

I pressed her. "My ba said I wasn't allowed to go to the forest or to Qing Qing's house. He didn't say I wasn't to go to the library."

Ah Fen was still hesitant.

I went on. "I have to do my homework and I need to look some things up."

She shuffled her feet for a while then said, "I'll go and ask him."

Worried that this might ruin my plans, I warned her against it. "You'd better not disturb him. You know what he's like when he's angry."

She hesitated again so I continued, "How about if I go and ask Nainai? If Nainai says yes, then you can take me."

Ah Fen was happy to follow Nainai's decision. What she didn't know was that I hadn't asked her at all. I'd simply walked up to Nainai's Buddhist shrine and come back again. I knew it was wrong—I was doing more and more bad things—but I had to get out of that suffocating house, and I didn't care how!

I wasn't a great reader and thought of the library as another stifling place. But Carola wasn't there, and that meant I could breathe freely. I looked this way and that, pulled out a book, then swapped it for another. After killing time in this way for half an hour or so, my eyes were drawn to a magazine. It was a magazine about archaeology, and there on the front cover was a photograph of a cloth doll just like Carola.

I rifled through the pages. There were more photos inside: of burial goods found in ancient graves by archaeologists, and of a mummy, a native Indian girl, her body dried out by the mountain wind—probably the same Inca girl that Uncle Ming De had told us about.

My eyes moved between the cloth doll and the mummy for a while. Then, with my nerves on edge, I started to read the article:

Child sacrifice was part of the important religious rituals of the Inca Empire. The Incas believed that offering a child to the gods was the same as sending the child to heaven, an act that could bring blessings upon themselves and their people. For this reason, many people willingly offered their own children.

On the day of the ritual, the chosen children put on adult clothing, which they believed they would grow into. They took two pairs of shoes, on the grounds that one pair would not be enough on the long road to heaven. They stuck a feather in their hair, and wore a spiny oyster necklace, the latter treasured as a symbol of the source of life. They wore silver bracelets and silver necklaces, and they took cloth dolls and little alpacas modelled in clay to keep them company on the journey.

When the ritual was over, the children would be led up towards the mountain peak, five thousand feet above sea level, surrounded by a crowd of people singing and dancing. They would frequently stop to drink and pray. Among the vast contingent were the people who drove the alpacas, the people carrying sacrificial objects, and the parents who had offered their children.

This part of the journey went on for many days, and included numerous rituals along the way. The higher they climbed, the smaller the crowd became, and by the time they reached the ice-covered peak, often only the priests were left. And there on the ice peaks, the shamans would carry out the final ritual. The children being offered to the gods were bound in a particular way and placed, together with their burial goods, in vertical pits three feet deep.

The children's faces are extraordinarily calm. It is sometimes said that they froze to death on the way. Some people say they were given large quantities of alcohol during the ritual, and others say that the high-altitude oxygen deficiency made them lightheaded. Whichever it was, their faces show no sign of their having suffered.

When they died, the children's souls did not go to heaven, nor could they return to the human world. Instead they were left to wander across the snow-covered peaks.

After many, many years, the Inca empire died out. The Spanish came and went and grave robbers started to poke around on the mountain peaks. They grabbed the burial goods, but weren't interested in the historical value of the mummies. Some cut through their clothes with a knife; others left them exposed in the snow. It was a sad state of affairs. It was so tragic you wanted to look away.

While the grave robbers were helping themselves to as much as they could carry, the child-souls wandering in the mountains seized their chance: they slipped inside the cloth dolls that had been buried beside them, and went *back to the human world with the grave robbers.*

So that was it! Carola did not have magic powers—she had been taken over by a child-soul! A shiver ran through me and my eyes drifted back to the photograph. I wondered if Uchu had been a grave robber. Otherwise why did he have so many of these old cloth dolls? Was this the reason he lived on his own in such a remote place and didn't interact with the villagers?

I desperately wanted to talk to someone. I searched the library for a familiar face, but there was no one. I needed to calm down, but my mind and body wouldn't listen—instead my hand followed my eyes as they scanned the bookshelf. I didn't know what I was looking for, but I felt there must be another lead somewhere.

Suddenly my eyes were drawn to a magazine displayed on the South American shelves. I took it down, flicked through it and was gripped by one of the articles.

A man whose business had failed had spent what little cash he had left on a cloth doll, from a flea market, as a birthday present for his son. It looked so different from a brand-new doll that he decided to tell his son it was an antique. He didn't want his son to know that he'd gone bankrupt.

On his way home, the man was involved in a car accident.

As he and the cloth doll were lying in a pool of blood, the doll started drinking his blood. The man was taken to hospital where doctors were unable to do anything except report that he was in a critical condition. In the depths of night, when all was quiet, the cloth doll climbed on to his bed, and whispered in his ear, "Baba, Baba..." The man thought it was his son calling him and glanced back from the edge of death. When he opened his eyes, the doctors were amazed—everyone thought a miracle had happened.

A few days later, the man left the hospital and the cloth doll told him its story. It was a child-soul from the ice-capped mountains and had drifted about the snowy peaks for several centuries before slipping into the body of a cloth doll, and heading into the nearest town with a grave robber. In the town, it had been passed from one person to the next, till it ended up in a second-hand shop.

As the doll told its story, the man listened in terror.

"Don't be afraid," said the doll. "All I ask is that you take me with you, and I'll help you get back everything you've lost."

The man was stunned. He didn't know what to believe. He was suspicious of the doll's claim that it could help him recover his wealth. "If you really have special powers, why did you end up in a second-hand shop?"

"Before I met you, I had found a body, but I needed blood to give me life. The car accident provided the opportunity.

I drank your blood and that's why I can talk to you now."

"Does it have to be human blood?" the man asked.

"Not necessarily, but human blood is the best, and it lasts the longest. But don't worry, next time you can give me any blood—a cat or a dog is fine."

The man was still in a state of shock when a woman walked past, and the cloth doll began to speak. "How lovely you are, Madam. You have the elegance of a lady and the innocence of a child. You are the most beautiful woman I have ever seen."

The woman's face lit up and she said to the man, "Why, thank you for the compliment! You are a superb ventriloquist."

Her words opened up a new world for this man.

When she had gone, the cloth doll boasted, "I can make you an amazing ventriloquist and help you recover your wealth. But you must promise to always keep me by your side and to love me as you would your own child."

The man promised.

Together they performed all over the world, and wherever they went their shows sold out. The man became famous and earned a fortune. He was happy and he kept his promise, treasuring the child-soul like his own son. They were very content together, until the day they went home. When the child-soul saw how close the father and his son were, he was fired with jealousy, and used his *special powers to try to destroy their relationship.*

I finally understood why Carola hated me so much.

12

Cats Attack in the Night

After my visit to the library, I was more unsettled than ever.

Whenever I closed my eyes, the image of the mummified girl would drift into my mind. There was still hope in her pure, child-like face, and the slight curve of her mouth gave the suggestion of a smile. Her hands and feet were pulled inside her clothes as though she were cold. I couldn't help thinking that the chosen children must know they hadn't gone to heaven, that they would be disappointed, and that it was no wonder we could still feel their malign presence. When I thought about it like that, I couldn't help feeling sorry for them.

I felt sorry for them, but at the same time I was afraid of them. I dreamed that Carola had become a real child. She wore my clothes. She held Baba's hand. She hopped and skipped on her way to school. At school, everyone called her by my name, and even Qing Qing couldn't tell the difference. I was desperate to tell Qing Qing not to be taken in by her. But I couldn't move my feet, because I had become a cloth doll.

I woke up in a fright and leapt out of bed. I was so relieved to find I could still walk, that I was still a real child.

It had only been a dream, but I became more and more convinced that the child-soul occupying Carola's body was going to kill me, pretend to be Liur and become Baba's real child. For a few days I was like a bird being preyed upon. I trembled with fear. I had no appetite. During that time, Nainai rarely came downstairs to eat. Ah Fen said she wasn't feeling well. Then Nainai's condition deteriorated and Ah Fen asked Uncle Ming De to come over. While he was with Nainai, I stood by the door, watching.

"It's nothing serious," he reassured her. "The medicine will make you feel better." Then the conversation turned to me. "Liur's so pale. She doesn't look well. Would you like me to see her too?"

Nainai called me in. He looked at me with a frown. "You're thinner than last time I saw you. Are you eating properly?"

I answered quietly, "It's too hot. I can't eat anything."

He furrowed his brow. "Are you sleeping well?"

I didn't say anything.

"She has nightmares," said Nainai.

"What's the matter?" asked Uncle Ming De.

I still didn't say anything.

Very gently, he said, "If there's something bothering you, it's better to talk about it, then the nightmares will go away."

I looked at him. I wanted to tell him about Carola, but Nainai was there, and I didn't dare.

He continued, "Qing Qing's gone to her other grandmother's. She'll be home next week. When's she back, come over to ours, OK?"

"I'll have to ask Baba." I spoke so quietly, I could barely hear it myself.

"I'll speak to him. Don't worry."

Then Uncle Ming De and Nainai started talking about the hospital, and I slipped out of the room.

Although Nainai's condition wasn't serious, Ah Fen was kept busy looking after her. One minute Nainai wanted a glass of water, the next she wanted her sutras. If it wasn't one thing, it was another, and Ah Fen was constantly on the go. I took advantage of the situation to sneak out of the house when Ah Fen wasn't looking.

Stepping outside, I felt like a bird uncaged. I flew off to the forest with a smile on my face.

There was an alluring fragrance to the forest that day.

Through the dense leaves, I could see red-stained clouds in the west and a flock of swallows flying over from the town. I stopped in front of Mama's grave, quietly enjoying the warm, soft sunshine.

Someone had been tending Mama's grave. I didn't have to guess who—I knew it must be Baba. What exactly were his feelings towards Mama? Love and longing? Or guilt and regret?

Was it only because of Carola that he was such a stranger to me? Or was there another reason? My eyes were brimming with tears as I asked Mama these questions.

And then I apologised to Mama. If I hadn't kept quiet about her illness back then, perhaps she might still be alive. Mama answered as she always did, through the sound of the wind in the forest. A cool breeze ran over my shoulder, like a gentle hand stroking me softly. I knew she was not angry with me.

"Don't worry, Mama. I'll look after Baba," I promised her silently, and ran off towards the marshes.

A rose-coloured ribbon of cloud was floating across the sky, and there was the sound of water in the distance. I felt an indescribable joy. Soon I was running, crunching over the dead leaves on the ground.

When I reached the deep part of the marsh, I saw my favourite duck. I longed to stop and play with it, but I was afraid of losing track of time, so I went once around the marshes, then ran back to the forest. I was skipping towards Mama's grave, when I saw someone kneeling in front of it. I didn't need to see his face to know who he was.

I decided to go another way round, so that Baba wouldn't see me. But my feet took me to the graveside. Slowly I walked up to him and looked at him in silence.

Baba turned around. He was flustered. Before he could say anything, I started to speak.

"I know I shouldn't come, and when we get back to the house, you can punish me—but don't send me away from her grave. Please don't drive me away from her grave. I haven't been to see her for a long time. I miss her, and I'm sure she misses me. Please let me stay a while!" When I saw Baba's face soften, I stepped closer. "It's been a long time since the three of us were in the forest together, and it must make Mama happy." I looked him in the eye and said, "I'm happy too. I've waited so long for this moment."

Baba had still not made a sound. He didn't move from Mama's grave.

This forest had once been our playground, filled with our joy and laughter. *We'll live happily ever after in the forest,* I had told my mama, believing it with all my heart. But after she died, everything changed. The forest became a memory of my lonely childhood, and since

Baba returned, it had become a forbidden place.

Why did the human world have to keep changing and upsetting everyone?

Baba's face was full of sadness. I dared to step closer. "Mama would never blame you for not saving her life," I said quietly.

I was just about to reach out to him when Carola sprang from behind him at lightning speed. "Who said you could come outside?" she roared. I stepped back, and that vicious look in her eyes drove fear into my heart again. "You are such a disobedient child. Get back inside —now!" she shouted, her shell bracelets grating with that ear-piercing sound.

I ignored her, and summoned the courage to say, "Baba, it's not easy for the three of us to be together any more. Don't let her get in the way or Mama will be unhappy."

"Your ma died a long time ago. What are you trying to do? Stir the dead?" Carola shouted furiously. "I'll tell you one more time—so listen carefully. Carolo is mine. He's not your baba. Your beloved baba died a long time ago. He died with your mama. Do you understand?"

"That's rubbish!" I roared at Carola. "If he was dead, why would he come to Mama's grave every day? He's come to assuage his guilt, hasn't he? Don't think I don't know. He killed her, and it was an accident. I'm right—I know I am. My ma died in his hands. I'm right, aren't I?"

Baba jerked as though he'd been punched, and fell to a crumpled heap on the gravestone. I hurried over to him, but Carola blocked my way, "Go away! Go away! He doesn't want to see you. Go away!"

"Baba, I'm sorry. I didn't mean it. Please don't be angry. I'll never say such things again. I'm sorry, Baba, I'm sorry…"

Baba hid his face behind Carola. It was true: he didn't want to see me. I knew I had hurt him, but I hadn't meant to. It was Carola's fault for provoking me. I begged him over and over, "Baba, please don't make me go. Baba…"

But he wasn't listening.

"GO AWAY! GO AWAY!" shouted Carola.

I stood up. I felt as though I'd been stabbed in the heart. I turned and ran, my face wet with tears.

All day, I wanted to apologise to Baba—but I didn't know how to. It made me so unhappy. But that evening, I forced myself to be calm—I knew I needed to be alert. Everything was still, all sounds frozen in the depth of night. All I could hear was the sound of my heart beating.

After a while, I heard Baba's voice in the room next door. "Now she knows I killed her mama, she'll never forgive me." He sounded so hurt.

"If you have to blame someone, then blame your old man. He was the one who forced you to do the surgery.

You can't blame yourself." Carola's voice was full of outrage.

"She wouldn't understand."

"She blames you. But perhaps you should be blaming her? She was with her mama every day—she would have known she was ill, but didn't tell anyone. So really *she* killed her mother."

"She was just a little girl," said Baba. "I was a doctor—and if I didn't realise she was ill, then how could I blame Liur?"

"She's bad. Why are you still protecting her?"

"She's my daughter!"

"She's not the sweet-natured little girl you used to know. She's changed. She's like her mama, always putting pressure on you. That whiny, needling voice of hers—it's awful."

I had no idea that was how Baba thought of me. My mind was churning away and I didn't hear what else they said—it was a minute or two before I honed in on Baba's voice again.

"If only the little boy had lived, everything would have been OK."

"How could it have been OK? With such a big burden upon him, that child would never have been happy."

"You're right; he wouldn't have been happy. He would have lived like I did—given endless encouragement, but so many boundaries. That kind of life is suffocating. But I often think that if the child had lived, Liur wouldn't be so isolated."

"Liur this! Liur that! If you're going to keep going on and on about her, then I'm not going to talk to you."

"Carola, why are you so angry? Remember, she's my daughter!"

"She is not. She's not your daughter. I am your daughter. She won't leave you alone—and she'll end up hurting you. I'm the only one who can make you happy. I will always be here by your side—here to comfort you."

Baba did not say any more. He just sighed.

"Carolo, remember what you promised me…"

"Now you're needling me too."

"I don't want to, but you're not keeping your word. You're just stringing me along."

"Give me a couple of days—"

"No! If you won't do as you promised, then you can't blame me for being rude to her."

"You mustn't hurt her."

"Then let me become a real child. Now! Do it now!" Carola commanded.

"I'm too tired. Tomorrow."

Baba didn't say any more, and neither did Carola. The night returned to silence.

The night passed with painful slowness. My eyes did not

close once, and I could feel my heart racing. I wondered what it would be like if the baby had lived? It was true that Yeye and Nainai would have been happy, and Mama wouldn't have been so tense. And if Mama had stopped being so stressed, then maybe she wouldn't have fallen ill. And if she was still alive, then Baba wouldn't have gone away. Apart from me, everyone would have been happy. And no matter how left out I might have felt with a baby brother in the house, it couldn't have been worse than this. After all these years, I could now see how important that baby was. We could have been a happy family... I let out a sigh. It was too late. Maybe it was like Nainai always said: *It's fate. Everything's determined by fate.*

The next evening, I found myself once again in a state of apprehension. I waited, trembling with fear. I had a feeling that something terrible was going to happen.

I leaned over my desk to watch the crescent moon peep over the tops of the trees and rise slowly in the sky. It had just reached its highest point, and was about to start its descent, when I heard the faint sound of a flute.

As before, Baba was at the front, playing and leading the cats up the path. Carola was on the ginger cat's back, her shell bracelets swaying as they moved. Behind them were the wild cats from the forest. They came very close to the house, then turned and headed away again, doing a whole tour of the forest before coming back to the garden.

Then Baba sat on the ground and the cats obediently sat down too. Carola climbed from the ginger cat's back —and I couldn't believe what I saw next. I blinked hard, thinking I must have been mistaken, but when I opened my eyes, there it was again. She had changed out of her clothes, and was wearing the jumpsuit I had worn on my third birthday!

I had such strong memories of that jumpsuit. Mama had wanted me to wear a pretty party dress, but I was determined to wear the jumpsuit. I remember telling her that I wanted to be a boy so that Nainai would love me more. The jumpsuit wakened so many memories, and reminded me of the pressure I had felt that year.

It shocked me to see Carola wearing it.

Up above, the moon was dazzling like a clear glass ball, spilling a silver glow over the dark earth. It lit up Carola's face, and her excitement and anticipation were clear. While Baba played on, she started to dance: a light, airy dance, graceful and elegant. My eyes followed her every movement, and it was as though as I was watching myself from all those years ago.

After she had danced in the moonlight for a while, Carola picked up a willow branch, went over to the cats and began to dance around them in a strange way, muttering as if she were putting a spell on them. It seemed to work, for the cats slowly got to their feet and started to dance to the same rhythm as Carola.

In just a few leaps, they approached Baba, stopping right in front of his face as he sat on the ground. Baba put down his flute and the cats stopped moving.

Then Baba pulled something out of his breast pocket. When I realised it was a knife, I nearly screamed.

Baba held the knife up in front of his face. It glinted in the moonlight. He stared at it, its profile as clear as a paper-cut silhouette. What was he going to do? My mind was racing, and I found myself shaking uncontrollably.

Before I had time to think, Baba had stuck the knife into his arm and a column of blood was spurting out, glowing red in the moonlight. Carola was trembling with excitement. She leaned towards Baba and, like a baby at the breast, drank the blood from his arm.

Finally Carola raised her head, her lips shiny and red, her glass-bead eyes sparkling like never before. She started to dance around the cats again. Each time she leapt she would turn and smile at Baba. The first time, I felt nothing—but the second time, it made my hair stand on end. A cloth doll couldn't possibly smile. I was shaking all over, staring at her. The third time she turned, the profile of her face was beginning to soften. The fourth time, her face was smiling and full of life, like a real person. My eyes were wide open. I simply couldn't believe what I was seeing. The next time she turned, her eyes suddenly turned fierce and she shouted, "Someone is watching us!"

She spun round at top speed and screeched wildly. Quick as a flash, the cats were heading straight for me. I cried out in terror, stepped back and fell to the floor. The window was only partly open, which blocked the cats from entering—except for one. As its claw shot out, poised to tear at my face, I put out my hand in defence, and a searing pain ran through me.

I screamed and then blacked out.

13

The Battle

I opened my eyes and found I was lying in bed. I felt weak and my arm was badly scratched.

"Those cats are evil. Attacking like that. It's shocking," Ah Fen muttered by my bedside.

"Carola told them to attack me. I've discovered her secret—"

"Not this nonsense again!"

"It isn't nonsense. If you don't believe me, go and look at Baba's arm. He cut himself with a knife." I sat up, buzzing with excitement.

"Your baba was trying to protect you. Have you any idea how badly you might have been injured last night, if he hadn't heard you shouting and chased the cats away? Those cats are vicious, you know. They scratched his arm very badly. There's a deep, long gash. He lost a lot of blood!"

"Are you saying he was hurt while he was trying to protect me?"

"Exactly! If it wasn't for your baba, your young life would be over."

"But that's not how it was. Baba cut himself. I saw it with my own eyes."

At that moment, I saw Baba coming into the room, with Carola in his arms, still wearing my clothes.

I screamed at the top of my voice.

Ah Fen put her arms round me and held me tight. "What's the matter?"

"Get out! Get out!" My whole body was shaking. I buried my head in my pillow.

"But it's your baba!"

"Get out! Get out!"

By the time I had calmed down, Baba had gone. Nainai had come in, and Ah Fen told her, "She's delusional. She must have had a terrible shock."

Nainai looked very frail as she sat at the side of my bed. Silently, she looked at the scratches on my arms.

"Should we call an exorcist? Or Dr Ming De?" asked Ah Fen.

"We already have a doctor in the house." Nainai's tone was cold.

"He was just here, but Liur took one look at him and screamed like she'd seen a ghost." Ah Fen realised she had said the wrong thing. She hunched her shoulders, and looked embarrassed.

Nainai looked at me. "So you're scared of your baba? What's going on?"

"It's Caro—" I closed my mouth and swallowed the words. Nainai wouldn't understand. Helpless, I turned over and buried my head in my pillow.

Suddenly there was the sound of a cat miaowing outside, stirring up my fear all over again. I screamed and curled into a ball.

Nainai took my hand in hers. "We've fitted an iron grille. Those cats won't be able to get in."

I looked at the window, saw the new grille and breathed a sigh of relief.

"Your baba called someone to come and install it."

"Baba did that?"

I was in a state of alert the day after the attack, and that, combined with the dull ache from the wounds on my arm, kept me from sleeping. Deep in the night, I heard voices talking in Baba's room, and although they were faint, they made me tremble with fear.

"Those cats are useless. Tell Carolo to kill them!" It was a voice I had never heard before.

"Let's deal with the girl first. As soon as she's dead, I can take over her body. I've had enough of this useless cloth doll. It can't walk, can't move. I'm completely dependent on Carolo. I'm sick to death of it." That was Carola.

"Carolo would never agree to it, would he? She's his daughter!" It was the unknown voice again.

"But *I'm* his daughter! I've drunk his blood. Now we're truly father and daughter. When the girl's killed, of course Carolo will be upset, but he'll get over it. He'll soon forget about her."

"What about the rest of the family? And her friends? Will they notice?"

"They're all idiots. The girl's told them so many times, but no one believes her. This is my chance. I can't let it go by."

"Auntie Carola, when you're human, you will help me, won't you? I don't want to be stuck in a cloth doll's body for ever."

"The girl has a good friend. I'll help you take over her body."

Now I understood. The voice belonged to the other cloth doll that Baba had brought back from South America. It was two-thirds the size of Carola, and nothing special to look at. I'd only seen Baba take it out once or twice. The rest of the time it stayed in his suitcase.

There was not just the headache of dealing with Carola, there were two of them! What's more, they were planning to attack Qing Qing. I had to think of a way of stopping them—but how?

All night I lay awake worrying, and finally fell asleep as day was dawning.

When the midday sun streamed through my window, bright and hot, I was still in bed. I heard Ah Fen calling me, and then Baba's voice. I didn't want to open my eyes. If Baba was in the room, Carola must be there too. I knew she wouldn't dare harm me inside the house, but still the atmosphere in the room was heavy and suffocating. I could barely breathe.

I heard Baba's voice again. "You can't stay in bed all day. I'll take you out for some fresh air."

I panicked, like a bird hearing the twang of a bowstring, and gripped Ah Fen tightly. "I won't go. I won't go."

Ah Fen flapped about with her hands and feet as she tried to comfort me. Baba watched me for a while, and then, not knowing what to do, he went away.

The following few days I stayed in bed. The scratches on my arm had already scabbed over, and Ah Fen was no longer keeping an eye on me all the time. As soon as she had gone, Carola would appear.

"The smallest scratch and you spend all day in bed. Not scared of losing face, huh?"

I didn't utter a sound.

"Poor Carolo, having such a lily-livered daughter!"

I stuffed my head under my pillow. I was boiling with

rage.

"Carolo, we can't let her stay in bed all day. If she doesn't get up tomorrow, we must think of a solution."

Carola was going to deal with me. I was scared, but I realised that I could no longer hide. Fighting Carola was the only option left to me.

The showdown came sooner than I expected.

Six days after the run-in with the cat, Nainai was ill again. She wanted Baba to examine her, but he insisted they call Uncle Ming De. They started arguing. It was probably anger that caused Nainai's shortness of breath, which affected her heart and caused her to collapse.

Nainai and I weren't close, but I was scared she might die, and insisted on going to the hospital with her. Baba ignored my pleas. Tears flooded down my face—until I realised there was an opportunity waiting for me. Baba and Ah Fen would take Nainai to hospital; they'd be gone for hours. It was perfect timing for a showdown with Carola.

Outside Baba's room everything was bright. Inside everything was dark. The curtains were drawn and a candle, flickering in a bowl on the altar, filled the room with ghostly shadows. In the weak light, I saw a cloth doll on the altar.

"Our enemy has come." I recognised the voice. It was the cloth doll that had been talking to Carola the other day.

"I've been waiting for her a long time." Carola's voice sent a shiver down my spine.

I followed her voice. She was lying in a hammock. "I knew you'd come." She sat up and, with an evil smile, said, "Let the battle begin."

My throat was too dry to utter a sound. All I could hear was my own chaotic breathing. My legs seemed to be glued to the ground. I was unable to move.

Carola leapt down and slowly made her way towards me. I glanced at the hammock again and froze. Shadows squirmed on the ceiling like snakes and centipedes, and a snake dangled down, its mouth open, showing its blood-red forked tongue. I was scared out of my wits, but I didn't run away. I had to seize this opportunity.

There was a click as the door closed. Carola's eyes were now focussed on the altar. The cloth doll by her side was looking askance at me.

"She's not as lily-livered as you think, Auntie Carola. We'd better be careful."

"I knew she'd come!" Carola grinned. "I've been waiting such a long time…"

My heart had almost stopped and I was struggling to breathe, but I could not give in. "I'm not scared of you!"

Carola laughed coldly. "We want to see what you're made of."

I threw myself at her, but in the blink of an eye she dodged my attack. My elbow banged on the altar, catching my scabs, and it hurt so badly that I yowled. Carola and the other doll laughed out loud and started dancing about. The shrill sound of shell scraping against shell sent me into a rage. I threw myself at Carola again, but she was too quick. Once again, I hurled myself into empty space.

The dolls circled me, spinning round and round, until I was dizzy. I took a few steps back, pressing my back against the altar. They carried on dancing, the scraping and grating of the shells louder than ever. I put my hands over my ears. I felt my head was about to explode.

Two rays of light shot out from Carola's eyes. Her mouth was open and drops of fresh blood were emerging from her lips. She was closing in on me, one step at a time. With my back against the altar, there was nowhere I could go. I curled in on myself.

I knew I was finished.

Carola launched her attack. I grabbed hold of the nearest thing I could find and threw it at her. She dodged, then there was a pause, and I risked a glance. Carola was looking at me. With a cold laugh, her voice grating horribly, she said, "Carolo's never going to love you again when he sees what you've done."

That's when I realised that I'd thrown a candlestick.

Fire was spreading throughout the room. I wanted to put it out, but Carola stood in my way. She didn't seem at all afraid. She danced above the inferno. In the glow of the flames, her lips looked moist with fresh blood, and she sang in a language that I couldn't understand.

In the blink of an eye, the fire had reached the tapestry hanging on the wall. The flames were licking like tongues, and in no time the whole room was engulfed by fire. I was trapped. The fire was burning so fast that I couldn't breathe—but I was not going to give up now. I hurled myself at Carola again. And she dodged again. She swayed about in the firelight, laughing "When you're dead, I'll be Carolo's real child."

I was caught in a sea of fire. I knew I'd lost; I had no strength to fight. Before I passed out, I heard shell scraping on shell, and Carola's ghostly voice. "My dream has come true! From now on, I am Liur!"

14

Becoming a Cloth Doll

I didn't die.

When I came round, I found myself lying in the hospital. My legs were wrapped in gauze. They hurt so badly. I heard Ah Fen asking anxiously, "Why did you set the house on fire?"

My throat was so dry I could barely get a sound out, but I had to explain. "I didn't do it on purpose. Carola and I had a fight. I grabbed the nearest thing and threw it. I didn't know it was a candlestick. And then the fire started. I tried to put it out, but she blocked my way. She wanted me to burn to death. It's all Carola's fault—"

"THAT'S ENOUGH!" Baba roared. I hadn't noticed that he was in the room. "Have you gone mad? You set the house alight and now you're talking nonsense." He turned and walked away.

Mad? Baba had said I was mad!

Ah Fen looked at me blankly, then she followed Baba out of the room, saying she had to go and look after Nainai.

I didn't care that no one stayed with me. I was used to being alone. But I couldn't bear the idea that they thought I'd done it on purpose. Arson was such a big crime.

Quickly my thoughts turned to how the battle had started. I tried to piece it together: I'd fallen, I'd been surrounded by fire—so who had brought me to the hospital? Had she escaped? Clearly, I'd lost the battle. Yes, I was still alive, but—as Carola had said—after the blaze Baba would never love me again. Nainai was bound to be angry too. Feelings of loneliness and vulnerability surged within me, and combined with the pain in my body. I began to cry.

"Liur, where does it hurt?" I hadn't seen Uncle Ming De come in. I wiped away my tears. "It's lucky you ran out of the room in time, otherwise you'd be charcoal."

My heart skipped a beat. The fire had been raging furiously—how could I have run outside?

Uncle Ming De looked at me hesitantly. "Would you tell your uncle what really happened?"

I glanced at him, then closed my eyes.

"Get some rest," I heard him mutter, "and let me know when you are ready to talk. If there's anything you need, just press the call-button on the bed-head, and a nurse will come. I'm going to see the other patients now. I'll come back and see you later."

When Uncle Ming De had gone, tears flooded down my face. If only Baba cared as much as he did.

The next day, Qing Qing turned up unexpectedly. "Mama said your house caught fire. What happened? Are you all right?"

Seeing Qing Qing, my spirits were raised for a while. I didn't want her to see that I'd been crying, but there was nothing I could do. I stared at her through eyes drowning in tears.

"What on earth happened? How did you set the house on fire?"

Qing Qing spoke gently, but it made me feel sad, and it made me feel guilty. Yeye had built the house himself and I had destroyed it. I had been through so much, but no one believed what I said. What was I to do?

Qing Qing's mother came to see me, and again I wouldn't say a word.

I heard Qing Qing say, "Ever since her baba came home, she's been acting very strangely, but I don't know what's happened exactly."

I had hoped that Qing Qing would understand me, but when I heard her say that, I resolved to keep my silence.

Ah Fen came to see me every day. I would lie in bed

with my back to her. I wanted to know how Nainai was, but I didn't ask. Baba didn't come again. Maybe it was for the best. If we didn't see each other, neither of us would get upset.

Qing Qing and her mother came to see me a few times, but I pretended to be asleep.

I didn't know how badly burned my legs were—they were still wrapped in gauze. The scabs on my arms itched, but I couldn't say they hurt. The worst thing was the nightmares—Carola would be mocking and taunting me. I would try to drive her away, but she had some kind of magic power over me. I would wake with a shriek and cry until my tears ran dry.

I would cry myself to sleep.

Uncle Ming De was very kind to me. He checked my wounds himself, and told me jokes. I knew he wanted me to open up and tell him my feelings, but I wouldn't let him go there. Sometimes he'd tell me what the weather was like outside, what was happening in the town, and sometimes he told me stories. And when he'd finished, he patted me on the arm and went quietly away.

One day he brought me some coloured pens and some paper to give me something to do when I was bored.

It didn't seem to bother him that I didn't touch them. He carried on smiling. Qing Qing was so lucky to have such a lovely, kind father.

During that period, I often thought how much better it would be if Baba hadn't come home. I would still receive postcards from him. I would miss him; but no matter how far away South America was, the distance between us wouldn't be as enormous as it was now. I would feel like I felt about Mama: I could still feel her near me, as though she'd never left.

All of a sudden, I remembered something that Mama had said. *When two people's hearts grow apart, there will be a distance between them, even if they are living in the same house.* At the time I hadn't understood, and it was only after this incident that I began to see clearly what she meant. Back then, I monopolised Baba while he neglected Mama. Now Carola was monopolising him. Was it punishment for what I had done? But what was wrong with a little girl wanting her father's love? I didn't believe that Mama could be angry with me for that—or she wouldn't have doted on me so much before she died.

If Baba had neglected Mama, he was to blame. How could it be fair for me to be punished for something he did wrong?

The more I thought about it, the angrier I became. I picked up the pen and started to scrawl on the paper.

When Uncle Ming De saw what I had done, he asked me, "Are you drawing yourself—or Carola?"

I realised that I was drawing a composite. Carola *and*

me. It was my face on Carola's body.

"Would you like to be Carola?" he asked.

I looked at the drawing. I was shocked and angry. I swept the drawing to the floor, screaming as I did so.

How could I draw myself as Carola? I might be jealous of her, but I didn't want to be a cloth doll, manipulated by someone else. What was wrong with me? The more I tried to think clearly, the more my head hurt.

The following day, Uncle Ming De came to examine my injuries. "They're healing nicely. There'll be scars, but it won't affect your walking. You'll be able to go home soon."

When I heard the word "home", there must have been a look of panic on my face. Uncle Ming De looked at me sympathetically, as though he knew I was carrying a burden, but he didn't say anything.

After he'd gone, I found a newspaper on the table. I didn't know if he had left it on purpose, or forgotten to take it with him. I glanced at it half-heartedly, and saw a terrible headline:

RIVALRY BETWEEN GIRL AND VENTRILOQUIST'S DOLL LEADS TO HOUSE FIRE!

Uneasily, I started to read.

Not long ago, the ventriloquist Carolo returned from overseas, and astonished everyone with his superb skill as a ventriloquist. As we might expect, Carolo treasures his partner Carola, his ventriloquist's doll from South America.

But, his doting on Carola made Carolo's daughter, Liur, unhappy and jealous. One day, when her father was not at home, the daughter sought her revenge. Her plan was to burn the doll, but the fire grew out of control. She destroyed the family home, and almost lost her life...

I was so angry, I couldn't contain myself. I roared and screamed, and ripped the newspaper to pieces. Uncle Ming De charged in, threw his arms around me, and tried to comfort me. Through a haze of tears, I howled, "They don't know anything. How could they write this rubbish?"

"Unless you say something, how can people know what really happened?"

"I did say something—but no one believed me. No one—"

"If you tell me, I will believe you."

I looked at him dubiously. He nodded firmly.

"Whatever I say, you'll believe me?" I asked.

Uncle Ming De nodded again. I could see in his eyes

that I could trust him. I softened. I told him about waiting for Baba to come back and then I told him everything that had happened since he'd been home.

When I had finished, I looked at him nervously. "Now do you believe me? Carola wants to hurt me!"

15

Memory's Eye

When Uncle Ming De told me that Baba was going to pick me up from hospital himself, I did not dare to believe it.

"Why hasn't he been to see me?" I asked.

"He's been very busy sorting out the house. Your yeye built that house and your baba wants to restore it exactly as it was before. That's not an easy thing to do."

I learnt that after the fire, Baba had rented a place in town as temporary accommodation, while he set about restoring the family home. Nainai had been discharged from hospital, and Baba had had to look after her as well—there was no time left to do anything else. Uncle Ming De was very convincing, but I still had my doubts. I was sure that the only reason Baba hadn't come to see me was that Carola still held a grip over him.

As soon as I closed my eyes, the scene of Carola

dancing above the fire would drift into my mind. She was wearing my favourite dress from when I was little, and had her hair in plaits, just like me. Even when the fire caught her skirt, she didn't move out of the way, but carried on dancing ecstatically. Having wandered for so many years across the snow-covered peaks of the Andes, why was she not afraid of fire? When finally I found the answer to this question, I couldn't believe how stupid I'd been: she was a soul. A fire could burn a cloth doll, but it wouldn't affect her at all.

The thought that I would never be able to get rid of her threw me back into a depression.

"Does Baba believe that the fire was started by Carola?"

"To be honest, I don't know," said Uncle Ming De, "but he understands that you've been jealous. He says that in future he won't talk to you through Carola, and that if you don't want to see her, he won't carry her with him all day."

My heart went cold. "He doesn't believe me."

"Liur, it's not important whether he believes you or not. The important thing is that you believe that he loves you. You need to get to know him again. Your expectations of him are stuck in the past, and you haven't seen the person he is now. Your baba's not a strong person, and he's changed a lot in the last five years. Even I barely recognise him."

Uncle Ming De paused for a moment. "He was hot-housed, overprotected, and put under tremendous pressure. He's gifted in the arts, but he was scared of going against your grandparents' expectations that he should be a doctor. He never dared to stand up to them. He wanted to create a new life for himself, but he wasn't strong enough. In this respect, he's very similar to the cloth doll in his hand—he needs other people to tell him what to do. In fact, he's only made one decision in his life. Do you know what that was?"

I shook my head.

"To marry your mama." Uncle Ming De looked at me. After a long pause, he said, "Your yeye and nainai were against the marriage, but your baba persisted. He courageously held out against them, until eventually they gave in. It's the most beautiful thing he has ever done in his life. It's such a shame that he didn't keep his promise to your mama. Back then, he told her that when they were married, if she couldn't get used to living in the family home, they would move out. They argued about this many, many times.

"He loved your mama so much, Liur, and he knew the pressure she was under—but he wasn't brave enough to remove her from the difficult circumstances. He felt such torment. He knew he had to get away, but he couldn't leave the hospital. And he hated being a doctor.

For others at the hospital, if their heart wasn't in their work, they could always do it perfunctorily. But not your baba. His weakness caused your mama pain. It hurt your nainai too, and your yeye was so disappointed in him.

"Your baba felt everyone was on his case, except for you. He told me once, you were the only thing in this world that made him happy, let him feel without pressure. He hid inside your two-person little paradise, thinking he could hide there all his life. He never imagined your mama might suddenly die. Her death was a huge blow to him. He didn't know how to deal with it, so he chose to run away. If it weren't for you, I believe he would never have come back. This alone is enough to show you that he loves you, isn't it?

"But he won't talk to me." My eyes were welling up again.

"What have I just said? It never occurred to him that you'd grow up. When your baba went away, you were still a little girl, always in his arms. That's the Liur in his memory. The sweet little daughter that he thought about every day was always in his head. He transferred his memories of those days on to Carola. When he came back and found you had grown up, and looked so similar to your mother, all those painful memories came flooding back. His entire being recoiled. This is how he has always been, recoiling at the slightest pressure. It's why your yeye was always angry with him, and why your mama was always complaining about him. We should be feeling pity for him.

"He always used to tell me that he'd have been much happier growing up in another family. Then he could have done what he liked. His situation constrained him —and his personality constrained him too. I thought he might have changed over these years, but he hasn't. His feelings are the same as they were five years ago. His little daughter of that time doesn't exist any more, and he doesn't know what to do. And he panics. Perhaps you do the same?"

Uncle Ming De glanced at me, his eyes so caring. Seeing there was no response, he carried on. "When your baba went away, you were still little. Back then, of course, you wouldn't have understood how complex adults can be. In the past five years, you've missed him and looked forward to him coming home. But your knowledge of him hasn't taken those five years into consideration; it hasn't moved on. No wonder he doesn't live up to your expectation. You're uncomfortable inside—that's understandable— and you're so very like your mama in the way you keep things to yourself. But the result is that you make things more difficult for yourself, and that's not helpful, is it?"

"I *have* spoken about it, but no one believes me!" Tears were flowing down my face again.

"You spoke about Carola's special powers, but not about your true feelings."

"I don't understand what you mean."

"Perhaps you didn't realise, but you've been projecting your psychological state on to Carola. When you said you couldn't stand her, you were actually saying you couldn't stand yourself. Right?"

My mind went blank. "I don't understand what you said—it's too complicated," I said defensively.

Uncle Ming De stared at me. "There is something knotted inside you that needs to be untangled, isn't there?"

I opened my mouth wide and was surprised that no words would come out.

"You don't have to tell me, and I don't need to know. But I want you to try and open up if you can. In this world there are no knots that can't be undone. Have a good think about it and you'll understand."

When Uncle Ming De had gone, I was all at sea, and that secret I had buried a long time ago suddenly came into focus. I was overcome with remorse—how could I go on living? I needed to be frank with Baba or this secret would trouble me for the rest of my life. I needed to talk about it. Even if Baba didn't forgive me, I still had to talk.

The day I was discharged from hospital, Baba came to

fetch me. We hadn't seen each other for over a month, and the distance between us was greater than ever.

With Uncle Ming De's help, a silent Baba pushed me in the wheelchair to the car park. Uncle Ming De opened the front passenger door.

"Let her sit in the back!" said Baba. "There's more room."

Uncle Ming De agreed, and helped me into the car. Then he laughed, "Liur, your legs haven't completely healed yet, so no extreme sport, OK?"

I nodded, and said emotionally, "Thank you, Uncle Ming De."

The engine started up. Baba still hadn't uttered a word. I looked at the back of his head and felt so ashamed, so apologetic.

I licked my lip, and called out "Baba", but he didn't seem to hear. So I leant forward against the front passenger seat, and was about to call his name again, when I saw her.

Carola turned to look over her shoulder at me. "We meet again," she grinned.

I froze with fear.

Before I could regain my composure, she added, "You're very lucky to be alive! Such a big fire. It's amazing you weren't burnt alive."

"Baba! Baba!" I cried in alarm.

He ignored me, concentrating on his driving.

Carola stared at me. I don't know whether my eyes were misleading me, or if she was using her special powers, but her body suddenly loomed large, until she was as big as me. She was wearing my favourite pink sleeveless dress over a white shirt. She picked up a headband from the seat and put it on. "I look just like you, don't I?" she said, laughing.

"Give me the headband." I reached out to snatch it, but she dodged my hand.

"All your things are mine now. It's not just your baba. Even your nainai and Ah Fen are mine now. While you've been away, they have accepted me as you. They've been lovely to me!"

"That's rubbish. Total rubbish." I was getting worked up.

"If you don't believe me, ask him." Carola turned to Baba. "Tell her that I'm your daughter now."

Baba didn't utter a sound.

"Is it true, Baba? Is it true, what Carola says?"

He still said nothing.

Carola jangled her bracelets. "Why won't you say anything?" she said angrily. "She killed your son, so why do you let her come home? Tell her to get out of the car."

How did Carola know my secret? I froze.

She targeted me with her eyes, and said with a

horrible smile, "You may be able to fool everyone else, but you can't fool me. As Uncle Ming De said, I am your psychological projection. Your secret has been revealed, and Carolo will never love you again. You've lost—well and truly lost."

"I didn't do it on purpose1" I cried. "I didn't intend for Mama to have a miscarriage! I was so angry that day and—"

"SIT DOWN, LIUR!" Baba shouted.

Carola gave a cold laugh. "It's true, you know. He'll never pay you any attention again." And she jangled my headband and her shell bracelets and made that noise that set my hair on end.

For a while, I struggled to breathe. "You're evil!" I managed to shout. I put my hand out again to grab the headband.

We started wrestling. The jangling of the shell bracelets made me even more outraged. I shouted and screamed.

And then Baba roared, "CALM DOWN, LIUR."

"You're telling me to calm down?! Why don't you bother about her!" I cried furiously.

I grabbed Carola's clothes like a lunatic. Her shell bracelets were jangling away. I climbed into the front seat, determined to rip the bracelets from her. She moved towards Baba, and I hurled myself at Baba's head too. The car shuddered violently and I was thrown into the air.

Everything went black.

When I came round, I felt something weighing down on me. I couldn't move and my entire body was in pain. I heard people shouting, "There's a girl in the car! Quick, get her out! Hurry!"

Someone was coming to rescue me. But I wasn't in the car… I was lying on the ground, with something pressing down on me.

The car. It had overturned.

"Quick, get the girl out of the car." The voices were urgent—but they were wrong. It was Carola in the car, not me.

Then I realised that Carola must have planned the accident. It was her chance to kill me and take my place once and for all!

I had lost. Totally lost. There was no more hope for me.

The pain was intense. It started deep in my heart and spread quickly through my entire body. I couldn't bear it.

Was this the end of my life?.

I didn't want to die, but I couldn't do anything about it. They were so busy rescuing Carola, no one noticed that I was trapped beneath the car. Worst of all, Baba was only inches away from me, and worrying about his Carola.

If he doesn't care about me, then living has no meaning? I said goodbye to him in my heart. *Adieu, Baba.* Tears were streaming down my face. I longed to see his face one last time!

I closed my eyes slowly and waited for Death to carry me away.

I saw Mama, smiling and wearing a purple cloak, standing in front of me. Had she come to get me? She reached out her hand to me and I ran towards her.

"Mama, Mama," I called as I ran.

But just before I reached her, I stopped. A little baby popped its head out from inside her cloak and smiled at me.

My balance went and I fell to the ground.

The baby was chuckling, and Mama said kindly, "Liur, he's your baby brother. Come and hold him."

"Mama, I'm sorry, I'm sorry," I howled. Tears flooded my face. "I didn't mean for you to collapse. I'm sorry, I'm sorry…"

The offence that I had hidden deep in my heart was finally out in the open. I had hidden it so deep inside me that I had all but forgotten about it. But it hadn't disappeared. It couldn't be made to disappear. I was the one who had caused Mama to fall.

I was the one who had caused her to lose the baby.

When Mama was pregnant, all her thoughts were focussed on that unborn child. She stopped singing for me, she stopped telling me stories. The house was filled with baby things, and she was filled with joy as she looked forward to the birth of my little brother. But I was filled with jealousy, and every time Nainai said, *If you're not a good girl, Mama will give you away when your little brother is born,* I became more and more upset.

One day, while resting after lunch, I wet the bed for no apparent reason. Mama was furious, and she said exactly what Nainai always said. If I wasn't a good girl, she would give me away when my little brother my born. I threw my toys all over the floor, which made Mama even angrier. My punishment was to tidy up the toys and stay in my room. But I didn't tidy up—in fact, I hurled the toys into every corner of the room. Mama had had enough of me. She turned and walked away. I kicked a wooden building block towards the door, and that's what caused her to trip.

I didn't know that if Mama fell, the baby would disappear; I was just so cross. When I saw her lying on the floor, moaning in pain, I was scared, and quickly called Ah Fen to take her to hospital. I had never imagined she might lose the baby.

After the miscarriage, Mama never mentioned how she had fallen, and I tried to forget about the incident. Maybe deep in my subconscious I felt guilty. I stopped clinging to her. And it seemed she kept her distance from me. After losing the baby, she was depressed, stricken with grief. She stayed in her room by herself, sinking lower and lower each day.

I knelt before Mama and begged her to forgive me.

She was still smiling.

Through my tears I asked, "Mama, do you blame me for what happened?"

She shook her head. She wasn't angry with me. I got up and followed her—but she floated off in midair, drifting further and further away.

"Mama, wait for me! Mama, don't leave me behind! Wait for me—"

"Liur, Liur…" I heard a familiar voice calling.

It was Baba. Baba was calling me. I had almost forgotten about him. Where was he? I wanted to call out to him, but my throat was too dry for any sound to come out.

Mama was standing in the distance waving to me, her lips moving slightly, as though saying, "Go back, go back."

And then she disappeared.

"Liur, Liur…" I heard someone calling me again.

I wanted to open my eyes, but my eyelids were heavy. I felt someone taking my hand. Was it Baba? Then I heard a voice saying urgently, "That's just a doll. My daughter's trapped under the car. Hurry! Please save her! Hurry!"

Then, there were lots of voices:

"That doll looks so lifelike!"

"Where's his daughter?"

I felt my hand being gripped tightly. I heard my name being shouted. "Liur, open your eyes. Look at me, Liur."

I struggled to open my eyes, and saw a face full of worry, eyes full of care. Those eyes are among the most beautiful things in my memory.

"Baba…"

"Liur…" He gripped my hand, two lines of tears rolling down from the corners of his eyes. There was blood on his face. I wanted to ask if he was badly hurt, but no sound would come out of my mouth.

He held my hand and said, "Liur, keep strong. We're going to get you out very soon."

I longed to talk to him, but the only noise that would come out was *Agh… Agh… Agh.* I summoned my last drop of life and gripped his hand. His face went blurry behind my tears, and very gently he wiped them away. "Hold on. You must hold on. You can't leave me. You can't leave me like your mama did." Two tears rolled down his face. "What would I do without you?"

I wanted to comfort him, but I had no strength left. My eyelids were beginning to droop. Baba was still talking to me, but his voice was starting to fade in and out like the wind.

"Liur…" He kept his grip on my hand, kept calling my

name.

Finally I felt someone moving my body and heard someone say, "She's seriously hurt, I'm not sure…"

"Why is it taking the ambulance so long to get here?"

"Is there a doctor?"

My eyes flickered open. The voices were drifting, floating towards me like little bubbles, and then—pop —they were gone. Goodbye, Baba, I said silently in my heart.

"I'm a doctor. I can save her."

It was the last thing I heard before I lost consciousness.

16

Afterword

I spent another four months in hospital. Baba had also been hurt, but his injuries weren't serious. He came to visit me every day. We didn't have a big emotional conversation or the dramatic hugs and tears you see in the movies. He was still as shy as before, and every time he came, he would just sit there, silently gazing at me. From the look in his eyes, I knew that this was the Baba who had loved me before.

It's not easy to make up for a gap of five years, and getting to grips with your childhood emotions is harder still. But I didn't lose heart. It was just as Uncle Ming De had said: I was no longer the little girl I had been. I had to treat Baba in a more mature way. I had to get to know him again, and not insist that he be the same father that I had been waiting for.

When my condition was stable, I told him the secret I

had been harbouring for years. I was afraid he would be angry and blame me. But he responded immediately: "It didn't happen like that."

And he told me what *had* happened. The baby was not affected by the fall. The doctor discovered that the baby was developing abnormally. If the pregnancy continued, the baby might die in the womb or put my mother's life in danger.

The news scared everyone, especially Mama, who had already found it difficult enough to conceive a son. Yeye and Nainai had struggled to accept the situation, but in the end the family had followed the doctor's recommendation to remove the child in order to save Mama's life.

Having lost the baby boy, the whole family sank into depression. No one had the heart to tell me what had happened: they thought I was too young; there was no need to tell me. For five years I had borne a secret guilt.

Baba was distraught to learn that I had blamed myself. When the truth was revealed, the knot hidden deep inside me finally began to loosen.

Uncle Ming De said I had managed to escape death twice, so I must value life more than any other person. He was right: God had been kind to me. I had survived two near-death experiences, and my soul had been saved too. I was lucky to have survived, lucky that my soul was saved. I was grateful to everyone around me.

By the time I went home from hospital, Baba had finished the work on the house, or rather the people he'd hired had finished the work. Nainai's health had improved, and she was so moved that he'd gone to great lengths to rebuild the family home that she gave up her grudge that he had not wanted to inherit the family business.

Would that be enough for our family to be able to get on and lead our lives happily?

I couldn't do anything about the issues between Baba and Nainai, but I wanted to improve the relationship between Baba and me. He wanted that too. With both of us trying our hardest, our bond grew closer. We went for walks in the forest, and, like before, I would tell him everything that had happened at school, down to the tiniest detail—and he would tell me about his experiences while travelling: what he had encountered, what he had seen and heard, just as I had hoped he would —except that we could not look at the postcards. They had burned in the fire. Baba wasn't upset; he had never expected me to keep them. He said he had sent them to remind himself that he was not alone in this world; that he had a family to go home to; that there was an address, a place that was waiting for him to return.

When he learned how much I'd treasured the

postcards, he was touched.

He added, "All the postcards I sent you were lost in the fire. Now it's your turn to send postcards to me."

"But I don't go anywhere." I didn't understand what he meant.

"I mean, when you've grown up, I hope you'll be able to make a journey like I did."

"You want me to go travelling round South America?" I looked at him in amazement.

"Yes, go travelling. Back then, every time I arrived in a new place, I would tell myself how much better it would be if you could be there too."

Tracing my father's footsteps had been my dream, and now it was a wish we both shared. I felt blessed, and told myself that no matter how difficult it might be, I must make this dream come true.

Although Baba and I were becoming closer, there was still another knot inside me. After the accident, I never saw Carola again, and Baba never mentioned her in front of me again—but as long as she was there, I knew we could never truly be contented or at peace.

One day, as spring was approaching, Baba and I went for a walk in the forest. The sun shone brightly overhead, relaxing us with its gentle warmth. The wind blew behind us, wafting the scents of the forest towards us. Wild rabbits ran in front of us, and the lilac, Mama's favourite, was in blossom. I was in heaven. Mama was right: as long as this forest was here, our happiness would last.

We arrived at Mama's grave, and in the light spring wind, we chatted with her about everyday things.

"I have to go away," Baba told her, "but I will come back to see you and our daughter often."

This time, I wasn't upset, because I knew he was going to do what Mama had urged him to do before she died: he was going to make a new life in his chosen field. He was a gifted ventriloquist, and I, too, encouraged him to pursue his dream—not try to fulfil other people's expectations of him. But I still couldn't stand Carola.

The next day, Baba left home. He was going to be on the road performing, and, like before, I would keep going to see Mama in the forest and keep waiting for his postcards.

Except this time Baba sent postcards much more frequently—and he even wrote letters! In the letters he would tell me in detail about the places he'd been, about the performances, and about his feelings. And I would write back to him. I didn't post my letters, because he was moving around. Instead, I kept them all in one place, to give to him on his return. Although he was seldom by my side, I felt very close to him.

By the time I went to university, Baba said he was too tired to travel and perform any more, and so he returned home. I was a student in a big city in the north, and only went home in the winter and summer holidays. I started to write to him from university, and sometimes I sent him postcards. I experienced for myself what he had spoken about—that for a traveller, having a postal address is more important than anything. When I started to send postcards, I would imagine the two of us travelling together in South America. But I couldn't help worrying—if Nainai died, who would we send the postcards to? I wrote this question on a postcard and Baba wrote back immediately, saying that we could write our home address, and when we returned we could share them with Mama—we would burn them, which would transmit them to her in the afterlife. It was a brilliant idea.

The thought of travelling with Baba in South America was so exciting. I couldn't wait, and suggested we go during the summer holiday. But Baba said it would be impossible to fit the journey that had taken him five years into two months; it needed at least half a year. He wanted me to finish my studies first, and to learn Spanish.

Then, when I was graduating, Baba fell ill. Within a year he had left me.

Before departing, Baba apologised over and over that he could not keep his promise to go travelling with me. But he wanted me to fulfil our dream no matter what happened; although he couldn't go with me, he would be up there watching over me.

He also told me that when he died I was to burn Carola.

I didn't do as he asked, but instead buried her with him. I didn't like her, but she had been with Baba all these years, and I wanted her and the person who adored her to be together for ever.

When Baba passed away, I packed my rucksack and set off on my journey to retrace his footsteps. Every time I arrived in a new place, just as he had done, I sent a postcard home, addressed to him and Mama.

My starting point was the medical centre where Baba had gone to pursue advanced training that year. From there, I headed south. When I got to Mexico, I visited all kinds of towns and mountain villages, and gained an understanding of the Indian peoples' cultures and customs. Then I went south to Belize, Guatemala, Honduras, Costa Rica, and from there into South America. I stayed in Peru a long time, and visited almost all the villages and hamlets in the Andes. All was going well, until I crossed the border into Bolivia. There, one day, I was wandering around a little town three thousand feet above sea level, and unexpectedly saw Carola inside a shop.

Shocked, I ran to the town square and sat on a bench to settle my nerves.

I laughed at myself for being so feeble. It was just a doll that looked like Carola—and yet it had scared me so badly.

I realised that although Baba was dead, and Carola was buried with him, the terror she had created in my mind was still there.

In the square there were lots of women with young children and babies, sitting on mats in the shade. The women wore traditional clothes, the children wore caps with earflaps. They played innocently until a traveller came along, then they'd gather round and put out their hands to beg. I knew to give them a friendly smile and send them on their way. But that day, my mind was all over the place, and when the children came up to beg, I was brusque with them and told them to go away. Carola still had a hold over me, and I needed to deal with it. If I kept suppressing the feeling, she would keep on disturbing me.

I sat for a while in the square, and when I felt calm again, I returned to the shop. There were many Indian dolls, all modelled like Carola, but all imitations. Although they looked the part, the craftsmanship and materials were much cruder. The shopkeeper asked me which one I liked and invited me to take a closer look. I could hear my heart pounding. I took a deep breath and pointed to one of them. The shopkeeper took put it on the counter for me to inspect. My hand hovered in the air for a long time, but in the end I didn't dare take it.

"How about a different one?" There was a strange twang to his Spanish, as though it were not his mother tongue.

"This one's fine." I forced a smile and, mind over matter, took the doll from his hand. I paid for it and quickly stuffed it into my backpack.

I went back to the square, found somewhere to sit down, and then took out the doll. Compared with Carola, it was really quite ugly; its eyes didn't shine; its lips weren't glossy, and the bracelets were just for show. There was no way they could scrape together and make a noise. Nonetheless, I was terrified. But I didn't want to throw the doll away, so I hid it at the bottom of my backpack.

When I arrived in Argentina, I bumped into Qing Qing. Well, "bumped into" is a bit romantic, because she had come out specially to meet me. She had told me that the postcards were beautiful memories of her childhood too, and so she'd decided to walk with me to "the end of the road". On my travels, I met lots of people, and hadn't felt at all lonely, but when Qing Qing joined me, I realised how wonderful it is to have a true friend when you are travelling.

I could imagine how lonely Baba had felt. Back then,

he was wandering around with a broken heart. No wonder he had became so attached to Carola. If he had transferred all his feelings for me on to her, perhaps he had transferred his feelings of guilt on to her as well? He'd created Carola as his alter ego. Carola was Baba. If I couldn't face Carola, then I would never be able truly to revisit the feelings of my past.

If I could not break that yoke, I would never be free from remorse. Travelling in Baba's footsteps to the end of the world was not enough to prevent me from slipping into an even deeper sea of bitterness.

My mother's death had been traumatic for Baba and me. We had both been in pain, but had not thought to seek help. Instead, we had tried to lessen the pain by running away from it. But we could not escape it; we had almost destroyed ourselves and those closest to us. Baba had left home in pain, and had spent his life wandering, never able to settle. I did not want a life like that.

When we were about to reach the end of the road, I pulled the Indian doll from the bottom of my backpack.

Qing Qing leapt back in horror. "What—?".

I didn't answer. I knew what I was doing: I was going to take it back for Baba.

Qing Qing looked at me in disbelief.

I smiled. "It's a shame she's so ugly. I wish I could have found one that was more like Carola."

Qing Qing's eyes were almost popping out of her head. But after a while, she understood—if I could do this, I could live my life without fear. She hugged me tight.

And there, at the end of the road, I healed the wounds in my heart—and I found my direction in life.

When I returned from my travels, I went back to university, and after professional training, I became a psychotherapist. With Uncle Ming De's help, I opened a clinic in the hospital, helping people who, like me, had experienced trauma.

At the same time, I worked on a plan to turn my beloved forest into a peace garden, so that my patients could have a peaceful environment in which they could enjoy the healing power of nature, just as I had in the past.

Made in the USA
Middletown, DE
05 February 2018